OMENS OF DARKNESS

VEIL OF SHADOWS

BOOK THIRTEEN

M. R. PRITCHARD

Paperback ISBN: 978-1-957709-61-1

About Veil of Shadows 13: Omens of Darkness

The Throne of Hell Awaits. The Final Battle Beckons.

Meg and Sparrow have faced insurmountable odds, but nothing could prepare them for the final descent into Hell. With Lucifer resurrected and chaos gripping the realms, they must rally their allies for one last battle to reclaim their kingdom and save their family.

But as the war unfolds, Lucifer delivers a shattering revelation: the curse Meg always believed marked Sparrow was hers to bear all along—a dark legacy that now threatens their daughter's life.

The stakes have never been higher, and as Hell's throne hangs in the balance, Meg and Sparrow must summon every ounce of strength, love, and sacrifice they possess. Because this time, the fate of more than one world rests on their shoulders.

The epic conclusion to the *Veil of Shadows* series will leave you breathless.

ONE

MEG

HEAVEN HAS NEVER FELT comfortable to me, and today is no different. It doesn't matter that I'm blood-bonded to the most powerful Angel in the Seven Kingdoms of Heaven; comfort has escaped me, and it seems I am back to searching for something that feels like home. Again.

I sit in Sparrow's living room, tracing the intricate designs carved into the armrest of an old wooden chair. I wonder if it's salvaged from his father's home–that would make it pre-Fast-Zombie War. This place is too quiet, almost eerie in its stillness. I wish Rue and Remington were here with me but they went to explore. I try letting the tension drain from my shoulders. Having my children nearby helps, at least we are in the same realm again.

I need to sit Rue and Remington down and discuss Sparrow with them. Maybe after that I won't feel so tightly wound. I've held on to this secret for too long and it's been eroding me from the inside. I just want to be free of it. The children are old enough to manage the truth. Although, I'm still worried about Remington's safety. He looks too much like Sparrow to keep his heritage a secret in this place.

The front door creaks open, the sound startling me out of my thoughts. A woman steps into the room. She is tall, her hair a cascade of golden waves that catch the light and make her look like the ethereal creature she is. She's wearing a white dress that clings to her curves, downy white wings stretching as she takes another step. A smile plays on her lips as her eyes scan the room, until they land on me.

"Oh," she says, her smile fading. "I didn't realize Sparrow had company."

My jaw tightens. Something about her presence ignites a fire within me, a possessiveness I've been trying my damndest to ignore.

"Who are you?" I ask, voice sharp. I don't bother to hide my annoyance.

She blinks, taken aback by the venom in my tone but she recovers quickly, giving me a smile too sweet to be genuine.

"I'm Lyra. Sparrow and I go way back. I thought he'd be here."

Lyra. Sounds like a strumpet.

"Well, Lyra," I say, standing and crossing the room until I'm just a few feet from her. Damn she's tall. "Sparrow doesn't need anyone from 'way back' at the moment."

She raises an eyebrow, her smile turning sly. "Really? Because last I checked, he and I have unfinished business."

The challenge in her voice is clear, and it sends a surge

of irritation through me. Sparrow's old girlfriend is turning out to be a real bitch. I don't want her seeing my children. I don't want her around me. I want her *gone*.

"Whatever business you think you had, take it elsewhere," I say, my voice low and threatening. "Sparrow's not here."

She glances over my shoulder and down the hall. "I'll just go check his room. I know where it is."

"Don't," I warn. "Go."

Lyra chuckles, the sound grating my nerves. "Let me tell you something, sweetheart, you're not the first, and you won't be the last." She sighs, looking me up and down. "You don't look his type..." Her eyes narrow. "Wait a minute. Are you...?" she takes a few steps back.

I flash a smile. Sharp teeth.

"You're the biter." Her hands fly to her neck.

I smirk, remembering the time I flashed here and ripped Sparrow's *other* blonde girlfriend out of his bed and bit her neck. That was kinda rude of me. But I was searching for revenge at the time. Can't blame a girl for that.

I step closer, my eyes narrowing. "You're right. I bite." I snap my teeth.

For a moment we stand there in silence, the air between us crackling with tension. Doubt flickers in her eyes, her bravado faltering. I get the feeling she might have expected someone to be here but didn't anticipate me. Story of my life.

Lyra rolls her eyes as she steps back. "Fine. Whatever. He's all yours. But don't be surprised if he comes looking for me when things get boring. He *always* does."

That's it. I lurch forward and Lyra turns tail and runs

out of the house. I chase her to the doorway, my heart pounding with the thrill of it.

Lyra takes to the sky and something sinks in my chest. A phantom ache stretches across my shoulder blades. I'll never fly again. I watch her go. He'd be better off with someone like her, someone whole.

"DON'T FORGET," he whispers against my lips. "That I am your prisoner as well. And we have been chained when together and when without each other. It's been written in the stars, our souls are perfectly formed puzzle pieces. No one else will do for either of us. We will be invincible together," he reminds me.

A DARK FIGURE with black wings appears, following Lyra off the Raven King's lands. I cross my arms and watch. Jealousy boils through my veins. Maybe I should have bitten her. I lick my lips. If she were royal lineage it would give me some more time before caving and dragging my sorry ass to Sparrow's room to beg for a meal. My mouth waters at the thought of drinking from him then instantly dries at the thought of him with another female.

I rub my eyes. Heck, I was with Skeele for nearly fifteen years; I'm sure Sparrow was with someone. I glance to the sky. Or many someones. Can't blame him too much.

When they are out of view I pace the porch. The thought of Sparrow's old girlfriends hanging around pisses me off. I don't want anyone snooping around. I step off the porch and start walking toward Nightingale's cabin in the distance. Jed might have to lay more wards or show me where I could bury a body on Sparrow's lands.

Two

"Lyra," Sparrow called as he landed, boots hitting the ground mid-step. The air around him crackled with dark energy. Lyra has always been slippery, finding her way into places she didn't belong. But this was different—this was personal. And he wasn't going to let it slide.

The woman was trying to avoid him now, walking with long strides until Sparrow caught up and grabbed her upper arm.

"Stop running," he called out, his voice cold and sharp, slicing through the silence.

Lyra stopped but didn't turn around immediately. She waited, plastering a smile on her face, refusing to let all of Babylon think there was a problem. When she finally faced him, she turned pale at the sight of him. "Sparrow," she greeted, her voice light. She glanced at where his hand gripped her arm until he released her. "I knew you were fucked up, but you're keeping that thing in your house." She pointed toward Sparrow's lands. "How could you? The fallen Queen of Hell. It's disgusting."

"I'm not going to answer any of those questions," Sparrow said, eyes narrowing as he stared her down. "How did you get past my gates?"

She smirked, tilting her head. "You know me. I have my ways."

"That's not an answer." Sparrow growled, his patience wearing thin. "You've always been good at slipping through cracks, but you should not have been able to breach my lands. Someone helped you."

Lyra's spine straightened. "Your Legion let me in. I wasn't aware that I had been banished. I thought we had something." She reached toward him.

Sparrow caught her wrist before manicured fingers could touch him. "Things have changed."

"But she bit–"

"I know. I was there and it no longer matters. That was a long time ago." Sparrow stepped closer to her and squeezed her wrist. "Why did you come?"

"I wanted to see you." She searched his gaze. "I wanted to invite you out. We used to have fun."

Sparrow didn't trust her. There were plenty of female Angels he'd used for their bodies and their blood. He shouldn't have let his time with Lyra linger over the years. It had only created a problem. A promise she's assumed.

Sparrow said, "There's nothing between us. It's over. Ended a long time ago. Stay away."

Lyra batted her eyelashes before glancing up and down his body. "What will the girls think? They'll all be heartbroken. Some of us really thought you'd pick a girl to settle down with." Big eyes glanced in the direction of his kingdom. "It must be lonely in that big house all alone."

"That was never going to happen. You all knew it." He squeezed her arm harder and pulled her closer. "You have an agenda and I'm not going to let you get away with whatever game you're playing."

Lyra met his gaze; eyes like her father's pupils blown wide. Sparrow would warn the Archangel that his daughter had been snooping. She was probably spying for him. Sparrow was going to say plenty about it at the next council meeting.

"I have never trusted you." Sparrow's voice was dangerously low. "And I don't believe for one second that you came here just to hook up."

Lyra's expression hardened. "Maybe I was curious. Maybe I wanted to see what was so special about what you're hiding in there."

"This place," he said, tone icy, "is mine. And it's off limits to you."

"What else are you hiding beyond that gate?" Lyra tried to pull her arm back, but Sparrow had gripped her so tight it was causing bruises.

"None of your concern. Tell whomever you're working with."

"Protective, aren't we? What's the matter, Sparrow? Afraid I might tell the wrong people about your little secret? Afraid I might tell someone you have the fallen Queen of Hell hiding out in your kingdom? What other creatures are you keeping there? Babylon will have a field day with this. My father–"

Sparrow grabbed Lyra's throat and squeezed. Sharp teeth flashed as he dragged her close. "Now, listen carefully. You're never going to mention Meg being in my home.

You're never to mention her name or presence to anyone. And you're never to come here again."

He squeezed her throat tighter until her breathing ceased and her eyes turned red. "Nod or die."

Lyra was still.

"This isn't a game. If you value your life, you'll heed my warning. Stay out of my lands. Stay out of my life. And stay the hell away from Meg."

She finally made the slightest nod of her head.

He released the Angel woman and pushed her away, disgusted.

"Fine," she spat.

And then she was disappearing down the pristine walkway toward Babylon.

Lyra was a problem he'd been able to ignore for years. He'd ruin her if she didn't keep her mouth shut. Or... Sparrow followed after her, palm tapping the blade at his hip, mind set. She would die today. Too much was at stake.

THREE

The sky was painted in shades of deep purple and gold as the sun began to dip below the horizon. Thrush led the way through ancient cobblestone walkways of the Raven King's kingdom. Remington and Rue followed closely, their eyes wide as they took in the scenery surrounding them. It was a place that felt both other-worldly and strangely familiar, like a dream they had almost forgotten.

They reached a secluded courtyard, where the scent of blooming night flowers filled the air. The courtyard was overgrown, the design quite different from the newer buildings and walkways. The children recognized it as something forgotten and discarded, the perfect place to meet in private.

Thrush turned to face the others, his expression serious. "What do you think of this place?" he asked, leaning against a marble fountain that burbled softly in the background. The marble had turned green with algae but the water ran clear.

Remington shrugged, his gaze drifting toward the sky. "It's nice, I guess. But it feels... heavy. Like there's a lot of history here."

Rue nodded, her dark hair catching the last rays of sunlight. She shielded her eyes. "It's so different from Hell. Not as chaotic but still intense. There's so much power in the air. The sun is too bright."

Thrush made a face before sighing and running a hand over his short, white-blonde hair. "Yeah, it's powerful alright. It doesn't feel like home. But all this... it's not enough to keep me here. Not when your mother is headed back to face Alastor. I want to go home."

Remington crossed his arms, his brow furrowing. "You think she's really gonna leave us behind again?"

Rue frowned, her eyes narrowing. "Mother has always been about protecting us."

Thrush's cheek twitched slightly, betraying his unease. "I don't want to stay here and be useless. We need to be ready, all of us together is our best shot at defeating Alastor. Look at your mother; Alastor cut off her wings. She's weaker than ever."

"Shay said she is formidable," Rue whispered.

"Not if she's dead." Thrush reached out to touch Rue's shoulder. "None of us have ever seen her like this. She's different."

Remington glanced at him sharply. "You think we have a chance against him? I heard that Alastor is going to resurrect Lucifer. Do you think we can win against him? Against the original fallen Archangel?"

Thrush hesitated, then shook his head slowly. "I don't know. But I do know we can't let him destroy our home.

We can't let him kill your mother. We have to do something."

Rue glanced between the two of them, her expression conflicted. "I'm going to name him Lucipurr," Rue said, petting the tiny cat in her pocket. Talking about war and her mother made Rue uneasy. She'd been having nightmares about it all.

Thrush burst out laughing.

The kitten meowed in accepting retort to his new name.

A heavy silence settled over the group as they all considered the possibility of going to war. It was terrifying.

Thrush finally broke the silence, his voice quiet but resolute. "If it comes to war... we'll have to go. We can't let them kill her." He itched his shoulder. "If you'd seen how she looked when the Raven King brought her back the first time..." Thrush shook his head. "She looked dead in his arms, with her wings cut off and blood everywhere." Thrush paled at the memory.

"She's defeated Lucifer before," Remington said, "Noah told us the story of how she battled him in the sky before she had her wings. She doesn't need the wings to be strong."

"I don't want mother hurt again," Rue said. The kitten meowed in agreement.

The three of them stood in the courtyard in a moment of silence, the weight of their decision hanging heavily in the air. They were young, unsure of what the future held, but they knew one thing for certain–they would face it together. They would return to help Meg in Hell whether their parents liked it or not.

"They're going to try and stop us," Remington warned. He touched the runes on his chest before glancing at his sister.

"We'll have to prepare in secret." Thrush looked at Rue. "Can you do that without spilling the beans?"

Rue nodded.

———

"I'VE FASHIONED wooden swords from some sticks I found in the forest." Chel passed each of the children a weapon.

"What do you want us to do with these?" Thrush asked, his body bruised and dirty from a day training with the Raven King's Legion warriors.

"Continue your Hellion training." Chel gripped his blade. "There is no better time."

"I'm tired," Thrush complained. "I'm going to get something to eat." He walked away with plans of preparing to escape to Hell when Meg left.

"Wait." Chel grabbed Thrush's collar and dragged him back. He turned to Rue. "You've had the least training."

"Then she will join the Legion," a familiar voice said.

Chel turned to see Sparrow walking closer.

"The girl?" Chel asked. "She needs to learn the way of the Hellions. She is small. Weaker than the boys."

Rue gave him a dirty look and Lucipurr hissed from her pocket.

"All the more reason to send her to work with the Legion." Sparrow looked down at Rue, remembering how his sister Nightingale had never been trained in battle. She had been "too crazy," according to his father, and locked away. Sparrow wouldn't let his daughter suffer the same fate of being unprepared with what was coming.

Chel opened his mouth to argue but Sparrow said, "Come, follow me."

The Raven King's Legion training grounds were a sprawling expanse, filled with regimented rows of Angel soldiers running drills and sparring with one another. The air was thick with the rhythmic sounds of combat–swords flashing, wings flapping, and the occasional barked command from the Legion's seasoned trainers. Soldiers clad in gleaming armor moved in unison, their motions sharp and precise. Fresh dirt and sweat clung in the air.

The Raven King strode forward with purpose, his imposing figure easily commanding attention. Behind him trailed Rue and Remington, their eyes wide as they took in the sights and sounds around them.

Chel followed closely, his expression growing more tense with each step they took.

"I don't like this," Chel muttered under his breath as they approached. "Hellions and Angels do not train together."

"The rest of your Hellions died in battle with Alastor," Sparrow sneered. "It will do you some good to spar. You're the last that remains of her army. You don't want to be out of practice."

Chel snarled.

"They need to be ready," Sparrow replied, his voice firm but not unkind. "You know what's coming. We can't afford to be unprepared."

Chel clenched his fists. He knew the Raven King was

right but he'd known these kids since they were babies. He'd seen the bruises all over Thrush. "Training with the Legion is too much for them."

"If we don't prepare them now, we'll be throwing them to the wolves. They need to learn," Sparrow insisted.

As they approached the central training area, the Legion Commander—a stern-looking Angel with scarred arms and piercing blue eyes—stepped forward to meet them. His gaze swept over Rue and Remington, and he recognized Thrush, then Chel, before settling on Sparrow with a mixture of respect and unease.

"Raven King," the commander greeted, inclining his head slightly.

"These two," Sparrow said, gesturing to Rue and Remington. "I want them trained."

The commander's eyes narrowed as he looked at the young ones, his expression hardening. "These are not Angels, Sir. They're children. We train Angels here, not... outsiders."

"Outsiders?" Chel snapped, stepping forward with a snarl.

Sparrow raised a hand to calm Chel before turning his attention back to the commander. "These 'outsiders' are the future. They're as much a part of this fight as anyone else in this Kingdom. I want them ready for anything. They've lost too much time already."

The commander hesitated, clearly conflicted. "They're not like us. Our training is... rigorous. They're younger than the fledgling." He motioned to Thrush. "It could break them. Especially the girl."

"Then let it break them," Sparrow said, his tone cold

and unyielding. "Better they break here where we can put them back together. They break on the battlefield and it's too late. They'll train with the Legion, or the Legion can answer to me." Sparrow's brow rose as he waited for a response. He didn't rebuild his lands brick by brick to be argued with. He was the King. And if he had to, he'd remind his Legion that he was currently the most powerful King in the realm.

There was a tense silence as the commander weighed Sparrow's words, his jaw tightening. Finally, after one last glance at the girl, he gave a reluctant nod. "Very well. They'll receive no special treatment here."

"They don't need special treatment," Sparrow replied, his gaze steely. "They need to survive in a war against true darkness."

The commander pointed at Rue's pocket. "The animal can't stay."

Everyone turned to look at Rue as a tiny head popped out of her pocket and mewed.

Sparrow held out his hand. "Hand it over."

Rue sighed as she pulled the kitten out of her pocket. "You be good, Lucipurr," she whispered to the kitten. "Don't let him scare you." She kissed its furry head before setting the kitten in Sparrow's palm.

"Lucipurr?" he asked, holding in a chuckle.

Rue glowered at him, a threat if he ever saw one.

Sparrow held the kitten close to his chest and saluted Rue. "We'll be waiting for your return."

The commander turned and barked out an order, and a pair of Angels stepped forward to guide Rue and Remington toward the sparring rings. The two children exchanged a nervous glance but followed the Angels without complaint. Rue looked even smaller amidst the towering warriors. Thrush knew where to go and sighed as he walked onto the sparring grounds he so despised.

Chel watched them go, his heart heavy with worry. He turned back to Sparrow, thoughts of his sister coming to the forefront. Perhaps if Yelena had some training she wouldn't have been murdered. It didn't take him long to change his mind about training with the legion. At least they'd learn skills from each realm.

Sparrow walked away, his wings dragging on the stone walkway. He tucked the kitten into his shirt pocket and took to the air. He needed to speak with Jed. The half-breed was working on warding the Raven King's lands to keep wandering eyes out while Sparrow and Meg were gone.

The Veil was thin and while Sparrow and Meg would be returning to Hell shortly, he didn't want to risk the children being unprepared and unprotected. There were no allies left. While his lands were under shadow, Lyra had still found her way in.

Four

Teari kneeled next to the Deacon and began unwinding soaked bandages.

"There's something wrong," the Deacon said as he hissed in discomfort.

"The bandages shouldn't be soaked like this." Teari inspected the wound where his lower leg had been cut off just below the knee where he'd been bit by the dead while escaping Hell.

Gabriel was watching from a few feet away. He glanced at the Deacon's pale face and considered the ramifications of the last Deacon dying on his lands.

Teari's hands were glowing as she moved them over the wound. The Deacons were unlike Angels, Demons, or humans. There wasn't much on their biology in her books. She'd never seen one missing a limb–let alone injured–and wondered if that was the reason he wasn't healing properly.

Her hands stilled as she found a pocket of infection. Teari's eyes flashed open as she sensed the festering inside.

She moved to her medical kit and chose a long scalpel and more gauze.

"Have you been changing the bandages every day?" she asked the Deacon.

"I try," was the reply.

"There's infection. I must drain it," Teari warned. "You want to be knocked out?"

The Deacon glanced warily at Gabriel then his stump. "Just give me something for the pain."

Teari nodded before going to work. She did her best to numb him with healing magic but was distracted by the infection. She cut skin and muscle until she found the pocket and drained it. When she looked up again, the Deacon's eyes were closed and Gabriel had a hand on the Deacon's forehead.

"Finish," Gabriel urged. "We have much to discuss with him."

Teari focused her energy on healing the surrounding tissue and closing the incision she'd made. There was still some healing to do but Gabriel stopped her.

"He's antsy," Gabriel warned. "I don't want him trying to get out."

Teari looked up and closed her hands, halting the healing. She grabbed rolled gauze and began wrapping the nearly healed stump. "It seems unethical to keep him injured."

"Everyone has their purpose. Being the last Deacon, we have to keep him safe and make sure others don't find him." When Teari was done, Gabriel removed his hand from the Deacon's head and the man woke.

The mood was somber as Teari packed her supplies, leaving fresh bandages on the table near the Deacon.

Gabriel dragged a chair closer to the Deacon and sat, his wings folded neatly behind him. His expression was one of deep contemplation, his brows furrowed as he traced a finger over the intricate carvings of the chair armrest.

As the Deacon woke, strange archaic energy gathered around him like shadows.

"She's been pushed to the brink," Gabriel began, breaking the heavy silence. His voice, usually steady and strong, wavered slightly. "Meg has faced trials that would have broken lesser beings. But this... this is different. Alastor will raise Lucifer... they are not mere enemies. They will be forces of nature against her."

"She is without wings," Teari warned. "Meg's strength is undeniable, but strength won't be enough. She can't poof to travel from place to place at will. She's still recovering from Alastor hurting her and Skeele's death." Worry lined Teari's face.

Gabriel nodded. "They will prey on her weaknesses, on her fears. The psychological toll could be her undoing."

"It's not right," Teari said.

"She is the only one who can bring balance," the Deacon said. He leaned forward, his voice a low, gravelly whisper. "You underestimate the depth of their malevolence, Gabriel. Alastor and Lucifer won't just battle her, they will seek to corrupt her. They know her vulnerabilities–the ones she keeps hidden from herself. They will use every trick, every whisper, every shadow to break her." The Deacon cleared his throat. "She has been very close to complete darkness before. It wouldn't take much to flip the switch."

"She keeps trying to go it alone," Teari said. "She's denying mourning Skeele. And I sensed a bond..."

Gabriel's hands tightened into fists. "The odds are against her but we must have some faith." Gabriel knew of the bond and it was one of the few things keeping her from running off to face the pending war alone.

"Indeed," Deacon agreed, his tone laced with sorrow. "But we cannot intervene directly, not without tipping the balance. The fate of many hinges on this battle. Meg must face it, but we must be ready... for whatever may come." He inspected Teari's work.

Teari's eyes glinted with something that might have been pity, or perhaps fear. Meg was an unexpected friend. They'd spent years growing and trusting each other. Even after Teari's first impression and judgement, Meg forgave her, somehow.

The Deacon said, "We must consider all possibilities. If she fails... if she is consumed by the darkness... we must be prepared to face the consequences. And they will be dire."

Gabriel stood abruptly, his wings flaring slightly as if to shake off the encroaching despair. "I refuse to believe that she will fall. She's come too far, fought too hard. If the worst comes to pass, we will do what we must. For her... and the balance of the realms. Babylon is prepared."

Teari was uncomfortably silent.

Gabriel took note and focused on her. "Tell me."

"Her children," Teari said.

"Child," the Deacon corrected.

Gabriel's head tipped to the side like he'd been told a

secret he couldn't quite hear. "Repeat that." He held out a hand to pause the Deacon from interrupting again.

Teari took a calming breath before she spilled the best kept secret in all of the Seven Kingdoms of Heaven and Hell and the Earthen plane. She met Gabriel's gaze after.

"Heaven has never been so blessed." She paused, gathering her words on thick breath. "Thrush is not the only child born to the Raven King's heritage. It has been a long time since a child was born to the Seven Kingdoms of Heaven and now the Raven King's family bloodline has three."

"Thrush," Gabriel said. "And the girl. Rue." Regret filled his voice as he rarely saw the girl; Meg had kept him away with excuses. He blamed himself after his confessions during Meg's trial. He figured he was too desperate, too forlorn from the time lost during Meg's childhood.

"There is another." Teari smoothed a hand over her slacks, glancing between the Deacon and Gabriel. "There is a boy. Meg had twins."

Silence echoed.

"A boy..." Gabriel whispered. Large hands stretched across his knees and he gripped the fabric of his robe. "But he's half Hellion, like the girl."

"No," Teari said. "They are the Raven King's children. Both of them."

"This is... unexpected," the Deacon said.

"Sparrow has two children," Gabriel said, not believing.

"If you saw them, you'd recognize it. The boy is the spitting image of his father. It's like looking back in time," Teari said. "The girl resembles Nightingale."

"You never told me," Gabriel stood and paced, large

hands tearing through white hair. "Why would you keep this from me?"

"She forbade me from telling a soul," Teari said. "It was not my secret to disclose. I feel badly telling you now. Meg doesn't want anyone to know. She fears for the safety of the children. She's kept them hidden all this time."

"Eventually they will have to send all three to do their time as Hellions," Deacon said. "Or the family curse will resurface."

Gabriel nodded slowly. "They must go."

"And if Meg fails against Lucifer..." Teari started to say.

"The children will be in Lucifer's grip," Gabriel said. "And this goes beyond retribution. You saw what he did to Sparrow. This is a war upon the families of the Archangels. Lucifer has always worked against us." He rubbed his chin. "He forbade my relationship with Clea. He was the reason she ran. The reason she died. The reason Meg was lost to us for twenty-five years."

"The Veil is thinning," Deacon warned and it seemed like a redirection of the conversation. "You'd like to blame Lucifer but Babylon has blamed Meg since the moment she stepped foot in Heaven."

"The Archangels have never been absolute in their theories." Gabriel stopped pacing. "The thinning will get worse. There are no Deacons in Hell. The newly dead souls will continue to collect. Hell's power will continue to strengthen. The Veil will continue to thin until it spills out onto the Earthen plane."

"And the Veil between the Seven Kingdoms of Heaven?" Teari asked. "There is a threat of thinning here."

Gabriel shook his head. "Our realm has never been breached. Our Veil is strong despite the imbalance."

Teari stood and lifted her medical bag. She turned to the Deacon. "I'll change the bandage daily, unless something more dire comes up."

"Thank you." The Deacon bowed.

"We'll have to get you walking again soon. I'll bring prosthetics. It will take some time to get you standing comfortably again." Teari adjusted her bag, waiting for Gabriel to *poof* her out of the mountain. He'd never shown a soul the entrance to this place, and she doubted he'd ever show her now that she revealed she'd kept the secret of his grandchildren from him.

"When will she deliver the bones?" the Deacon asked.

"Soon, they'll leave any day now," Gabriel said.

The fate of many rested on the aftermath of the coming battles, but none more so than Meg. Her children were at risk. Her soul was at risk.

As they left the chamber, the lights dimmed as if the heavens were holding their breath, waiting for the inevitable clash between light and darkness.

FIVE

Jed knelt in the frosty grass, drawing runes of protection and warding on the stone wall at the edge of the Raven King's lands with practiced precision. Each sigil glared briefly with faint light before sinking into the stone, extending the invisible protective web stretching across the kingdom. Jed was nearly done with the southeastern perimeter, the most remote of Sparrow's lands.

Jed felt a shift in the air and turned.

The Raven King was walking closer.

"Your work's coming along," Sparrow commented, his gaze sweeping over the runes. "Looks like you're nearly finished."

"Almost," Jed said shortly, his voice low. He trusted the Raven King less than most, but like before, Jed knew hiding in Sparrow's shadow would protect him.

Sparrow gazed over the northern perimeter and sighed. "Can you work faster?"

"I am only one man," Jed said, "in a territory that would rather see me dead than alive." Jed glanced over his shoulder. "I have no plans to die here. For every rune and ward I set, I must check my back for danger approaching."

"You're safe here," Sparrow promised.

Jed gave a sarcastic smirk. "You've a Legion of Angel warriors who have tried to kill me since birth. At any moment they could turn on me. My runes and spells only go so far when they can see my face and aura lit up from using my magic."

Sparrow tilted his head, the ghost of a smile tugging at the corners of his mouth. "Still don't trust an Angel?"

"Trust isn't the word I'd use," Jed replied dryly, brushing his hands off. "They've had eons to perfect a lot of things, including the art of deception."

Sparrow crossed his arms and pondered. "I could find someone to help you."

"No thanks. I work alone." Jed tapped the stone wall. "These will hold up against most intrusions. But I'd still keep an eye out for anything from these parts."

"Is it strong enough to stop anything coming from Hell?" Sparrow asked.

Jed raised an eyebrow. "Worried about escapees from the underworld coming for a visit?"

Sparrow's expression turned serious. "Things are... restless. Everywhere. Babylon has gotten curious. I trust no one. Already had someone sneak past the gates."

Jed was eyeing the runes he'd tattooed on Sparrow's arms years ago. "Did they ever work?" he asked.

Sparrow shrugged, but it looked like he was holding in a neck tick. "I can't remember."

Jed and Sparrow made eye contact for the briefest moment before Sparrow turned and walked away.

Six

Sparrow paced the length of his bedroom, boots scuffing softly against the hardwood floor with each agitated step. The room felt stifling, the walls closing in as his thoughts twisted and turned. The hunger gnawed at him; he'd drank half the stock from the blood fridge and left the rest for Meg. He knew she'd avoid him, just like she had the past few nights. She was stubborn, and avoiding the hunger would do nothing more than put them both at risk. There was a deeper hunger though, not just for sustenance but for something far deeper, something that clawed at his very soul.

Something–no, someone–who had dark hair, marked skin, blue eyes.

Sparrow's thoughts were a storm. He wondered if she had told the children the truth. The boy had avoided him since the morning he'd made breakfast and Rue pointed out they looked alike. Remington had simply stared at the Raven King, watching him thoughtfully as he chewed, then cleaned his plate and left with Thrush at his side.

The uncertainty of a future with the children gnawed at him, fueling his restlessness. If they knew, would they look at him differently? Would they hate him for the darkness that shadowed his past, or the curse that haunted their very existence? Would they hate him for what he'd done to their mother? Sparrow shook his head. There were no easy decisions between Heaven and Hell and he doubted the children of this kingdom would have it any easier.

Sparrow's fingers flexed involuntarily, itching to reach for the door, fly to Babylon, and jump in the portal so he could get this mission to Hell over with. Lucifer's bones were the last piece of the puzzle, the final task. The weight of it sat heavily on his shoulders, pressing down with the remainder that every moment he delayed was a moment Meg and the children were left vulnerable. They would go in the morning. They couldn't wait any longer.

Meg had been grumpy, withdrawn, ever since Lyra's unwelcome visit the previous day. Sparrow could sense the tension in the air whenever they were near each other. He had tried to approach her, but words caught in his throat. He didn't want to discuss what he'd done the past fifteen years and with whom. He didn't want to hurt her anymore.

Sparrow rubbed his throat. He didn't want to push Meg too hard, didn't want to make things worse, but the hunger was becoming unbearable. The blood bond was a double-edged sword; it tied them together in a way that was both exhilarating and terrifying. A strength and weakness.

Sparrow stopped pacing, his hand resting against the wall as he took in a deep breath, trying to steady himself. He had the children to protect now, the kingdom to rule and grow, and dark alliances to maintain that would bring him power.

Sparrow raked a hand through his hair, frustration tightening his chest. He wanted Meg, needed her, but knew he couldn't force her to open up and let him in. And the thought of her getting hurt, of losing her again–he couldn't bear it. The memory of losing her once before was too fresh, too raw. If something happened to her now...

No. He wouldn't allow it. He couldn't.

A familiar twinge started at the base of his neck and he couldn't prevent the spasm from taking over. Sickness filled his gut. The random twitches were few and far between, a muscle memory as Teari called them. His mind was intact but too long without his memories resulted in this. The jerks and tremors never left his body completely. His hand curled into a fist as the spasm in his neck stopped. He rested his forehead against the cool wall until the twitching dissolved completely.

With a final sigh, Sparrow pushed away from the wall and walked to the door. He couldn't wait any longer. He had to see her and find some way to make things right. The hunger was too strong to ignore. He didn't trust himself not to seek her out like the days when he was a Hellion, with urgency and little regard for her safety. No, Sparrow couldn't wait. He needed Meg *now*.

The flooring outside his door squeaked.

Someone was there. A spark of recognition flooded his veins. Sparrow whipped open the door to startled blue eyes.

"Finally," he muttered, grabbing her arm, and dragging her inside.

Seven

Meg

Stumbling, Sparrow drags me into his room.

"I'm still mad at you," I say, pushing at his arm until he releases me.

"Stay mad then." His gaze drifts down my body. "Are the children asleep?"

"Yes."

I want to tell him that they know their real father is the Raven King. They seemed unimpressed, almost like they knew already. After, they settled into bed as though not much had changed. I'm not sure how to take it. Either they're resilient or smarter than I expected.

Sparrow's lips press into a thin line like he wants to talk more about them but decides not to. The discussion is due. Maybe I can ease him into it.

"Rue was grateful you didn't harm Lucipurr while she

was training with the Legion." I notice a scratch on his arm and press my fingertip to it.

"The kitten didn't like flying." He flexes his wings while stepping closer. "He will get used to it. If Rue plans on carrying him around in her pocket while she's flying."

"When will they get wings?" I ask.

"When the time is right," Sparrow replies. "There's no set age. They come when they've earned them."

I step away from him and rub my arms. My stomach growls loudly.

"You sent them to train without informing me," I say, holding back annoyance. "These are decisions you need to discuss with me."

Sparrow crosses his arms over his chest and looks down at me. "They must prepare. I will not have children of mine die at the hands of Lucifer."

I hold up my palm to stop him. "Slow down. Things are moving fast."

"They're about to move faster," he warns. "We must return to Hell in the morning. It's time to hand over the bones. This task is long overdue."

"Okay." I nod in understanding. "But don't think you're taking over raising my children. I make decisions about their safety."

Sparrow touches a rune on his arm. "Are you sure about that?" he asks. "Seems they've made plenty of their own decisions."

I exhale a breath and look up. Hair falls across his eyes but it doesn't hide the intense green stare. His wings shift. A man shouldn't look like he does. Handsome and dangerous, long lashes and high cheekbones. The dark runes tattooed over his arms and up his neck add to the dangerous aura of him. Who the fuck am I kidding trying to avoid him, he is everything I've ever wanted. Batshit crazy or unnervingly sane, I cannot deny the attraction to all of his personalities.

Sparrow rubs the back of his neck.

My stomach growls too loud.

He glances down with a smirk. "It's been too long."

He tips his head, revealing throbbing veins.

I lick my lips and take two steps back. "I can go hungry for days," I warn. "But if you're hungry, you could call that bitch Lyra to come back. She looked your type."

It's not nice of me to hold it against him. But I'm still angry she barged in here unnoticed. Who knows what she's spread around the Seven Kingdoms?

"You told me we'd be safe here and she just walked in the door like she lives here."

"She's been dealt with," Sparrow says. He takes a step forward. "She won't return."

"How'd she get in?"

"That's been dealt with as well."

"Is that what you prefer now? Tall and blonde and winged?" My back aches. I've never been good at backing down, and it's worse now that I feel weaker than ever.

He looks me over and moves closer. "Do you prefer horns and rough skin and sharp teeth? Do you prefer leathery wings, the filth of Hell in your bed at night?"

His mouth is so close, his breath fanning my cheek then neck as he tilts his head.

"I prefer those who hurt me the least," I say.

I notice the smallest flutter of muscle along his shoulder. I touch the spasming muscle and notice as Sparrow holds in a twitch.

"It's come back?" I ask. Unease tightens my gut and reminds me that I truly don't know enough about Sparrow's lineage.

His gaze meets mine. "It never truly went away completely. I just learned to hide it."

My jaw drops as I try to think of a response.

"I see the way your expression changes. Maybe that's what you like? You want me so fucked in the head I can't think straight. You like the crazy. Every day is a battle keeping it at bay." His smile is kinda sad.

No, I never enjoyed one minute of watching him slip away and forget me, forget himself.

"I should have known. Nightingale still has her quirks," I say.

He whistles a soft trill that sounds like a Wood Thrush at dusk.

"The thing about learning darkness, is that it helps me hide the ticks in the light," Sparrow says. "The hunger makes it worse, harder to control."

He stretches his neck and groans. He licks his lips and I realize the hunger makes us both mad.

"We must return to Hell in the morning. This ends tonight." Sparrow's hand glides up my arm.

I shiver as his palm smooths across my back and pulls me closer against his hard body. "Just to be clear," he says. "I prefer you in my bed. Always have."

Firm lips press to mine and my hands smooth up his chest and behind his neck. My veins feel lit with fire as his hands slide across my back and under my thighs. He lifts me and presses my back against the wall.

"You're so bad. Little night owl. Swearing at me and being jealous of other women in my bed." He kisses my jaw before his tongue swipes over my neck. "You can hate me for it. I've given you enough reason. I can't apologize for trying to survive without you. I can never say sorry enough." We both know this.

I feel the sharp slide of his teeth sending a shiver up my spine, but he doesn't bite.

"You can bring it up a million times," he says.

Sparrow's thigh settles between my legs and I can't control my body as my hips grind on him.

"I can't make you forget, I can only repent," he says as he pulls away. Disappointment reveals itself as a sigh from my lips.

"I told you I'd kneel to you every day. I'm overdue." He moves lower, ready to drop to his knees.

I pull at his arms. Tug at his shirt. "Please. No."

He stills. Dark wings spread.

"Please," I beg. "Please..." My stomach rumbles.

He reaches for the button on my jeans, pauses. "You want me? This? Are you giving me permission?"

"No," I whisper before slapping my hands over my mouth. The lies fall so easily from my lips. I want him more than ever. More than anything. I always have.

"You don't want this just like you didn't hide Lucifer's bones." Sparrow chuckles as he drags the jeans down my legs and pulls my boots off.

I feel his warm breath on my thighs and squeeze my eyes closed.

"Maybe tell me some truth. Let's start with that, Meg." He throws my bottoms aside.

I suck in a shaky breath.

"You make me wait for days. You ignore me. You turn my world upside down." He rubs circles on my thighs with his thumbs. "You bring me two heirs to the throne out of thin air. I'm due for a truth." Teeth nip at my thigh.

I let my hand fall away from my mouth. "I don't like that you slept with tall, winged, blonde women." I am so judgmental.

He rises up on his knees, grips the neck of my shirt and pulls down until it rips. "They could never replace your addictive darkness." His fingertips trace the ink on my arms, my shoulder, the damaged one over my heart. "They were nothing." He glances up at me. "I quit them a long time ago."

Oh, this is a sight. Sparrow on his knees, touching me, wings spread, veins pulsing, begging for truth. Those green eyes looking up at me.

What he said doesn't sound like deception.

"Make sure they remain as nothing," I say, bending to drop my lips on his.

Kissing Sparrow is like kissing a bolt of electricity. His arm snakes around my waist and pulls me to sitting down onto his thighs. I feel a bulge in his pants. Frantic hands tug at clothing.

"Too hungry," he mumbles, his forehead pressed to my shoulder. He whistles something that sounds like a hungry chickadee.

"What are you waiting for?" I ask, tugging at the waist of his pants and tearing his shirt open.

"Permission."

"Do it. Please," I say as I lower my mouth to his chest and nip until a small drop of blood appears. I lick it away as Sparrow's hands slide into my hair, grip at the root, and tip my head away, revealing the side of my neck. He flicks his tongue over my blood stained lips before his mouth falls to the sensitive skin below my ear.

"Why do you wait for permission?" I ask. "I thought we were beyond that."

"For all the times I forgot to ask," he says solemn.

There are memories of him being loving and kind, memories of him forgetting who I was and taking at will only to leave me drained to a husk. There were times when he drew blood and never asked.

This is better. Much better. My hips grind against him and a coiling starts deep in my belly. "Yes," I groan, biting my lip. "Please."

It starts like a simple kiss to my neck, until I crave the pinch of teeth like he craves my blood. But he takes his time working me up. By the time he presses teeth to my skin, I'm nearly gone. The pinch sends me over the edge, gasping and throbbing...

"We leave in the morning," Sparrow says. We finally made it to his bed and I realize with both of us lying here, it seems kinda small for two people.

Belly full and legs weak, I move to return to my room across the hall. Sparrow grabs my hip and drags me across the bed, tucking me against him. His arm wraps around my waist, holding me against his body.

"What will the neighbors say?" I joke.

"They'd say finally, if they had any sense." He presses his lips to the scars on my shoulders. "But I don't care what those assholes say."

Something fades inside me.

"You are mine and I am yours," he whispers the familiar words. "Stay."

EIGHT

Nero had never been one for patience. What horse has patience? There are no virtues for horses to abide by or, at least, none that Nero cared about. Restless energy rippled within him. His black coat rippled as he galloped through the open fields of the Raven King's kingdom, wind tugging at his mane, whispering ancient secrets.

Nero had searched the forests, the rocky cliffs near the coast, and the winding riverbeds, but the white horse he glimpsed days ago was nowhere to be found. Nero wondered if the white horse roamed the hidden corners of the Seven Kingdoms of Heaven, slipping between realms like a shadow in the night, like Nero had done between the Earthen plane and Hell.

Nero didn't think the white horse was a ghost, but what was the reason he couldn't find it?

Nero's hooves pounded against the ground as he raced through the fields, eyes scanning the horizon, ears perked for any sign of life. He knew the landscape well, from the deep pine groves to the scattered rocks of a burial site. But there was something off about the air today, an uneasy stillness clung to him like an omen.

With a snort, he slowed his pace as he approached the outer borders of Sparrow's lands, Babylon visible in the distance. The towering spires rose like jagged teeth against the sky, their golden surfaces shimmering in the fading light. He had heard Jed and Shay discussing Babylon, sensed revulsion in Meg's voice when she spoke of the ancient city. It was not a place he ventured lightly, but if the white horse had passed through here, he would have to take the risk.

Nero stopped for a moment at the edge of Sparrow's territory, his gaze narrowing on the dimly lit pathways of Babylon. He could feel the power thrumming in the air, saw the cages where the Archangels punished sinners underneath the blistering sun of Heaven. Nero knew it was a bad idea to leave the misty cover of the Raven King's lands. But, desperate times called for desperate measure.

Nero backed up, then with a deep breath, he galloped forward and leapt over the stone wall separating the Raven King's lands.

As soon as his hooves touched ground, he felt the pull. Something ancient, older than anything he had ever encountered; older than the Demons he'd come across since he became a Crossroads Demon. It wrapped around him, trying to seep into his bones. Nero shook it off with a flick of his tail and continued forward, his gaze sharp and focused. He should have known better; a Demon horse can't walk the streets of Babylon unnoticed. He didn't belong here, and Sparrow had warned them all to lay low.

He had offered them sanctuary, and Nero was sure he couldn't get back to the Raven King's lands should anything come after him.

His steps echoed as he moved through the deserted streets, the towering statues of Angels watching him from every corner. Despite the grandeur the streets felt empty, hollow, as if the city were waiting for something or some-one. Most likely souls–Babylon was starving for them since the destruction of the Safe Houses and death of the Deacons. All souls were stuck in Hell and soon the dead would start walking on the Earthen plane again.

Nero pressed on. He saw a glimpse of white from his periphery, and it turned to nothing but a hint of mist. But then... there was the faintest trace of a scent. He wasn't sure it was real at first–something that smelled like freshly fallen snow. He followed it, galloped at moderate speed, and paused to hear something other than the echo of his own hooves. Something pulled him to the edges of the city. Maybe it was instinct or maybe the call of the white horse. Whatever it was, it led him toward the towering gates of the kingdom bordering the Raven King's.

Nero paused, taking in the grandiose gate that shim-mered with celestial light. Nero paced and whinnied softly. He saw a flash of white again, raised his head, and watched between the gates. Something was running between the trees, teasing him, taunting him. "Chase me," he swore he heard the wind whisper.

Nero trotted in a tight circle. He didn't want to cause trouble, but the white horse was clearly beyond these gates.

Then, Nero remembered that he didn't care much what

others thought. He backed up and sprinted forward, leaping over the wall.

Nero huffed, his breath coming out in a cloud of mist. This would cause trouble he wasn't ready to deal with. Trouble that would come to Shay and Meg. Deep down though, Nero knew that they'd want him to find the white horse. And if not, too bad for them.

There was a shift in the air, and a low growl made his skin prickle. Nero froze, muscles tense. Shay had warned him not to take his Demon form while in Heaven, but he was all too ready. Two Angels from the Legion approached.

"Never seen a black horse here before," one of them said, stepping forward.

Nero's lips curled in a snarl, but he remained still, hoping they'd spill some information.

Nero whinnied, tried to relay that he was no danger. He nodded in the direction of the white horse.

"Passing through?" the other Angel asked with a smirk. "You saw the white one, didn't you?"

Nero nodded.

"Ah the white horse," the other Angel said wistfully. "Usually the young ones search for it. It's a kind of enigma around here." The Angel secured his weapon. "Seen wisps of it myself. Never the whole creature out in the open. Lore says she sticks to the shadows and only watches from afar."

She? Nero held in all movement. He wanted them to keep talking. Wanted them to spill more secrets.

"I saw it once," the other Angel said, holding his hand out to Nero.

Wonderful. Nero didn't come here for pets and snacks.

He was on the hunt and the longer he spent with these morons the further away the white horse would get.

Nero let the Angel get closer, then pulled away.

"Easy, boy. You want me to keep talking?"

Nero eyed the Angel, noticed the way the feathers of his wings fluttered with the night breeze.

"Okay. The white horse has been around for ages. Longer than anyone else."

Nero tipped his head and let the Angel pet his snout, then the sensitive scratching spot behind his ear. Nero was so invested in the story the Angel was spinning, he forgot to keep an eye on the other Legion guard. When Nero did glance over, the guard had a sinister smirk.

"Gotcha!" The Angel closest gripped Nero's mane.

Joke was on him. Nero reared up and kicked the Legion guard in the gut. The Angel went flying across the grass on his ass. The other one didn't dare approach after that move.

Nero took off in the direction he last saw the white horse. The faintest scent of snow hit his nose. He doubled down: Nero was faster than lightning, faster than the speed of light, faster than a black hole. Trees bent away from him before he passed them, hoofprints appeared in the soil before his gallop echoed. The ground in the distance shook before the black blur passed.

Suddenly, Nero was no longer in Heaven. He was on the Earthen plane.

He followed the smell of snow, ran across freeways and prairies and cornfields, until he saw *her* drinking from a half frozen lake in the middle of nowhere Utah.

The white horse.

"*Took you long enough to find me,*" the white horse said with a voice that was soft and strong and very female.

Nero huffed in surprise and took a tentative step forward. The Angel was right.

"*Speak. Demon horse.*" She bent to gently lap water from the lake.

Nero stared, unbelieving. He'd never spoken, only had the inner monologue that lived rent free in his head.

NINE

MEG

THE PORTAL to Hell rips open in front of us, a swirling mass of black and crimson that feels like it could swallow us whole. Our hands brush for just a moment before I step forward into the abyss. Sparrow hesitates for the briefest second.

The instant we cross through, the air changes. Brimstone and pine and... something smells off. It's different than the last time I was here, or maybe I didn't notice the drastic change when I came searching for the feather of truth. The sky looks smokey, a red tint to the clouds that hadn't been there before. Maybe this is the imbalance the Deacons always warned about. I swallow hard and tamp down the unease threatening to take over my body.

I glance at Sparrow, noticing the brief second in which his jaw tightens.

"It feels heavy here," I say, rubbing my chest with the hope of releasing the weight of Hell.

I adjust the strap on my pack and shoot a glance at Sparrow. "We get in, we get out. No distractions."

Sparrow nods, his eyes scanning our surroundings. "No distractions."

We walk, our boots kicking up clouds of ash and dirt as we head toward route 37.

Alastor's reign has changed this place. I don't recognize the landscape much here any longer, but the one thing I do know is that there is a barn on route 37 with a snowy owl in the rafters. Except there's no snowy owl any longer. All I have left of her are feathers in a jar, hidden away for safe keeping. Now there's just the bones. The bones of Lucifer.

"Why don't you just fly us there?" I ask Sparrow.

"The tone of Hell has changed." He shivers. "Can't you feel it?"

I nod. "I can tell."

"Give it time," he warns. "It'll get worse. But, we walk." He points his blade toward the road ahead.

"Can't we hotwire a Jeep?" My thighs are already sore from the short distance we've walked. Or maybe that's from riding Sparrow last night.

"The noise," he reminds me. "I have to save flying as our last resort. We aren't that far."

The route is familiar because we've walked it before, side by side in a different life when we were different people. Sparrow asks about Rue and Remm, about Thrush and the childhoods he missed. I never apologize for it. I never will.

He mentions little bits, asks about moments he should know nothing about. Like when Thrush fell out of the tree in the courtyard and Nero watching Rue like a guard dog whenever she took a walk alone. He shouldn't know those moments and it leads me to believe he had someone watching us all along.

Eventually, we come to a stop in front of a dilapidated barn on Route 37.

"You sure you remember where you hid them?" Sparrow asks, his voice low.

I give a sideways glance. "I remember. Not the kind of thing you forget."

"Right." He nods. "Just checking."

Sparrow keeps looking around us like he hears something. Like he sensed something lurking just out of sight.

"What is it?" I ask.

"I can't tell if it's undead, Hellions, or bored Demons," he says, fingers flexing on his blade.

He glances at me and I notice his eyes linger to my back.

Rage instantly floods me and I can't control it. He thinks I'm weak. "The barn is up here. We can split up. How about I go left and you can go fuck yourself?" I walk faster, eager for this journey to be over.

Sparrow catches up with me in a few long strides. He grabs my arm. "What's that all about?"

"I saw you... that expression of regret and disgust."

It hurt. A lot. Dealing with my loss of power and ability to fly is enough but having him look at me like that was unbearable.

"I'm simply analyzing how to keep you safe. It's not like you can fly away. Not like you can just *poof* out of here like you used to."

Dark eyes glance down the length of me.

"Unless it's all come back." He waits for a response.

"It hasn't," I finally say. "And sorry I'm such a hindrance to this bullshit mission." I pull out of his grip and head toward the barn. He's so focused on my weaknesses. I should remind him I endured twenty-five years of abuse on the Earthen plane and survived. I didn't need wings then or the ability to travel from place to place at will. It would have been nice, but I survived without it. Just like I'll survive now. I count on my fingers how many times I've nearly died. Three sounds right. If I were a cat, I'd have plenty more lives left.

I take a deep breath and calm myself as we stand in front of the barn.

"Where would you like me to wait?" he asks.

"In the shadows," I whisper, fanning the fingers of my left hand like a magician.

Sparrow makes a deep hooting sound from deep in his throat. His head ticks to the side.

I go still as stone. "You okay?" I ask.

"Fine." His eyes darken. "Get the bones."

I get the bones all right. I know exactly where I put them. I enter the barn, the rotting wood shifting under my boots as I walk across the bottom floor. I pause for a moment to make sure the rafters aren't going to fall on my head. Then I make my way to the back corner. A beam of moonlight illuminates where I left them. Slamming my boot down on a loose floorboard, I bend the wood up and away. There it is. A bag of bones.

Ten

A chill ran down Sparrow's spine as he moved closer to the broken doorway of the barn. They weren't alone. He knew it; he could feel it. His fingers twitched on the hilt of his blade.

Suddenly a screech echoed in the distance, growing louder, closer.

"Come now, Meg," Sparrow called into the barn. Her shadow moved as she ran toward him, the hollow clank of bones in her bag echoed.

Both Meg and Sparrow halted, exchanging a knowing look before their eyes shot to the horizon. Shapes were moving fast, the unmistakable figures of Hellions.

"Run!" Sparrow shouted, grabbing at Meg's arm as they bolted away from the barn and through the nearby field. "Head for cover."

Sparrow was faster, nearly dragging Meg. He'd counted four Hellions. It would be an easy feat to take them on, but he didn't want to leave Meg on the ground and he didn't want her falling out of the air and getting hurt.

The Hellions were gaining speed, quickly closing the distance. Sparrow's wings flared, but there was no space to take off, not without leaving Meg behind. He gritted his teeth, using his strength to pull her along as they dashed through the dry, cracked field. The forest loomed closer, shadowed fringe calling to them—safety was within reach.

There was another building in the forest. They skidded around the corner, the sight of a door sending a surge of relief through Sparrow's chest. They could hide.

"In here," Meg said, yanking the door open and diving inside.

Sparrow followed, slamming the door behind them. The guttural calls of the Hellions lingered over the forest canopy. Sparrow hoped they were as thick as the Hellions of Lucifer's time. All brawn, no brains. He pressed his back against the door, chest heaving.

It was a smaller barn, a decaying remnant; rafters sagging, the smell of rot thick in the air. In the corner, something small like a rabbit or raccoon was rotting.

Meg stood, wiping her hand on her pants. Sparrow hadn't seen her fall and moved to help her.

"We can't stay here," Meg said.

Before she could finish her sentence, the barn door exploded inward. Wood shattered, and a hulking figure stepped inside. It wasn't a Hellion—not this time. It was something equally terrifying. A dark, monstrous creature, its body twisted and malformed: a Demon. Its eyes glowed red, claws dripping with black venom.

"Shit," Sparrow muttered, drawing his blade in one swift motion.

The Demon lunged at them, its roar shaking the

ground beneath their feet. Sparrow shoved Meg behind him, swinging his blade in a wide arc as the creature's claws came down, barely deflecting the blow. The force sent him stumbling back, and the Demon's tail whipped out, catching Meg in the side, and sending her crashing into the barn wall. Her bag fell to the ground.

"Get out!" Sparrow shouted, but Meg was already on her feet, eyes blazing with fury.

"Not without the bones!" Meg gritted her teeth, her voice hoarse as she scrambled toward the dropped bag.

The Demon recovered quickly, roaring again as it barreled toward them. Sparrow darted forward, his blade slashing through the air, sparks flying as his blade collided with the Demon's thick, scaly hide. The creature was relentless, barely slowing as it swiped at him again, its claws raking across his arm. Blood welled, but Sparrow gritted his teeth, ignoring the pain.

"Go, Meg! Now!" he shouted, parrying another blow.

Meg didn't hesitate this time. She sprinted for the back of the barn, smashing through the rotting wood shoulder first, and disappeared into the night. Sparrow followed, barely dodging the Demon's massive tail as it lashed out. Sparrow created a bigger hole in the side of the barn as he followed Meg. They ran, the Demon close behind, the screeches of the Hellions echoing all around them.

There was no way they could outrun them all. They had to find another way out. Sparrow's mind raced, looking for an escape, any escape. He glanced to the sky. No. It was too early for that. The Hellions would take them both down before he could make it to Alastor.

"There!" Meg shouted, pointing toward a narrow crevice in the rock wall ahead.

It could work. Sparrow judged the width of his shoulders and wings. He'd make it work.

They dove into the crevice, squeezing through just as the Demon reached them, its claws scraping against the stone, too large to follow. Sparrow collapsed against the wall, breathing heavily, the distant howls of the Hellions and the Demon fading into the background.

Sparrow glanced at Meg, blood dripping from his arm, his face pale. "Next time, maybe just bury those somewhere a little less conspicuous?"

Meg rolled her eyes but couldn't suppress a small grin. "Next time? There will never be a next time." She glanced at the blood dripping from his arm. "You're hurt." She moved closer.

"I'm fine."

Meg noticed the black venom pooling in the wound. "Shit," she muttered, taking off her belt and wrapping it tightly around Sparrow's forearm.

"What are you doing?" Sparrow asked, and Meg thought his words sounded a little slurred. He slid to the ground.

"We have to get the poison out. I've seen this before."

She didn't have time to tell him the story of Shay and the Demon poison trapped under her scarred leg. The last thing she needed was an incapacitated giant to drag around. She didn't have magic to heal him and had to revert to old school human first-aid.

"Are you going to pee on it?" he laughed. "Or thuck it out?" His lips were drooping. Shit.

"Yeah," Meg said cynically as she knelt next to him. "Or I could let it infiltrate your bloodstream and turn you into a Demon. Sounds tempting." She lowered her mouth over the scratch marks. "I think you're halfway there already."

Sparrow whispered something that sounded like a curse word, equal parts worried and turned on.

She sucked the diseased blood and venom out of his arm then spit it to the side. She did this until she could no longer taste the venom only blood that she'd much rather swallow than spit on the cave floor. Then she pulled a bottle of water out of her bag and rinsed her mouth before pouring some water on Sparrow's arm.

"Does it hurt?" she asked.

Sparrow licked his lips and made no effort to alter his expression. "That doesn't hurt," he motioned to his arm. "Something else does." He smirked. "I'm suddenly quite hungry."

Meg gave him a dirty look before moving away and searching her bag for bandages. She returned to his side and moved his injured arm to her lap. Sparrow's hand closed into a fist as Meg wrapped the cuts with a strip of gauze and tape.

"You should consider armor," Meg suggested.

"Never needed it before." Sparrow was watching her. "Maybe something cool like Basilisk skin."

"You heal quick." She started to move away but Sparrow's hand gripped her wrist.

"I could heal quicker." He dragged her arm closer. "Wouldn't even need the bandage you just wasted on me."

Meg's eyes went wide.

Eleven

Meg

HERE? In this filthy cave? I search Sparrow's face for clarity. Yeah. He's serious. Embracing the Bloodlust in a Hellcave isn't high on my list. But he does kinda look pathetic all bruised up. I consider all my options: I tell him no, and we carry on with his arm injury and hope it doesn't delay us. Or, I tell him yes and I keep my teeth to myself and suffer with blue balls the rest of the trip. I'm not sure which sounds worse. It all sounds shitty.

Sparrow is still waiting, holding my arm as his head tips back against the rocks. He takes a deep breath, and his finger rubbing my wrist sends a shiver up my spine. There is only a sliver of light from a crack in the cave above us and I can't gain much from his expression, only the pained sound of his voice.

"Anything involving teeth is a bad idea," I warn.

"I'll be good," he promises, voice low. "Just a sip. Just a few drops. Just the tip... of my teeth against your neck."

"I'm not fucking you in a cave in Hell after we just ran from an ugly ass Demon and Hellion." I gently pull my arm away but he grips tighter.

"Please," he begs. "It burns."

"Fine." I scoot closer as he moves my wrist to his mouth.

I look away as his teeth scrape and I hold my breath, tampering down the Bloodlust that's bound to torment me within a few moments.

"Better?" I ask as he settles my hand on his chest, holding my arm like it's a beloved teddy bear.

Sparrow smirks something dark. "It really wasn't that bad. But your mouth on my–"

I punch him in the gut.

Sparrow groans and tips to the side, holding his stomach.

"What the fuck is wrong with you?" I ask, shaking my sore hand. It feels wet. I move to the light shining down from the ceiling of the cave to get a better look at my hand. It's covered in blood.

Sparrow drops to his side and goes silent.

"What the fuck?" I mutter.

"I was hoping you wouldn't notice," he whispers.

"We have been here for five minutes..." I drop next to him and pull his shirt up. "Why didn't you wear some type of armor? Don't kings wear leather vests or some shit?" I sit back on my heels and take in the deep scratches across his stomach.

"I don't need armor. It's just a scratch. Suck out the

poison," he says. "And then go a little lower." He shifts his hips and smirks.

I might kill him.

"Get your mind out of the gutter. If I didn't need you to fly me to safety, I'd slit your throat and leave you to rot in this cave." I reach for my bag. "I'm never going anywhere with you ever again."

The silence worries me as I search my bag for something useful. I glance at his wound. The edges of his skin are turning black from the Demon's poisoned claws.

"You have a healer you can call on?" I ask.

"I don't have a healer." He groans. "You're going to have to suck it out again." He scrubs his face.

"I think you enjoyed that too much." I shake my head. "You disgust me." I move closer, bottle of water in my hand.

"I know," he says. "I am vile and despicable."

"Keep going." I bend and suck the poison out of the first deep gouge in his stomach. I spit the sour blood to the side, worried that I'm not hearing his voice. That he might be worsening. "I'm not hearing you," I say, ignoring the way his tense stomach feels under my lips. Damn.

"I am horrific. An abomination." Sparrow's hands remain over his face, muffling his voice.

I clear the next wound and become concerned with the amount of blood I'm spitting to the ground.

"A disgrace," he says. "Something loathsome."

I pour a few drops of water over his stomach then rinse my mouth. The edges of his skin are turning back to pale pink.

"Make it sound like a prayer," I demand.

"A stain upon Heaven's gates. Detestable."

I continue removing the poison, the sharp taste in my mouth becoming bothersome. I pause to rinse with the water. Sparrow's face looks pale. A fine sheen of sweat collects in the hollows of his neck. I gaze a little too long.

"Don't stop. I have more," Sparrow murmurs. "Wicked."

I press my mouth to the last wound.

"Revolting." His voice is so low.

I spit to the side and internally agree with Sparrow's assessment of himself. I've thought all the same things.

"Without my grace I am nothing. I am hollow. My heart is dead." Sparrow lowers his voice. "But... I have you again."

"Shut up." I rinse his wounds then press fresh bandages to them. He's so quiet I think he might be asleep.

Sucking out the poison wasn't enough. He can't be walking around with a torn up gut. I bite my wrist then hold it over his mouth. His lips seal around the marks. He holds my arm like it's precious. His hips shift. Wings scrape against rock. I want nothing more than to climb on top and quell the deep ache in my center. But this is not the time.

It's not long before he's had enough. I pull my wrist close, then scramble away from him and deal with the blood lust on the opposite side of the cave, pacing like a wild animal in heat until it passes.

———

The cave's mouth looms behind us as we make our way out of the forest. I glance at the sliver in the rocks and wonder how we even saw it in the first place while running from the Demon and Hellion. Must've been a miracle.

Above us, the sky churns with thick, swirling clouds, casting an ominous glow over Hellscape.

I glance at Sparrow; he's moving like he was never injured.

Sparrow notices me watching, giving me a sidelong glance before wincing dramatically and holding his stomach.

"Shut up," I warn.

"I suppose I should thank you," he drawls, his voice rasping from hours of silence as he slept while his body healed. "For healing me. Though it felt more like you were trying to suck the life out of me in the process. You know–"

I smirk, adjusting the strap of my bag. Lucifer's bones give a hollow knock. "If I wanted to suck the life out of you, Sparrow, trust me, you'd be dead by now."

Sparrow gives a low chuckle, though his eyes flick with the same unease that had lingered on me in the cave. There's a heck of a lot of heat in that gaze and all I can envision is the sight of him adjusting his hips like his pants were too uncomfortable on that hotel couch.

"Right. Always the gentle touch, Your Majesty."

"Don't call me that," I snap, the words sharper than I intended.

Sparrow lifts his hands, fake wincing at the movement in his arm and stomach. "Easy there. No need to get testy. Just trying to show some thanks."

I narrow my eyes at him, but the tension slung between us is heavy, unspoken. I wanted to do much more than heal him once I got a taste of his untainted blood. And he knows it. Not trusting myself, I move away from him. Nothing's better than distance in a situation like this. I know I'm short tempered, especially like this. Doesn't matter if we're dragging these bones back to face a war. I'd still knock him over in the woods and take what I want. So I move even further away.

We head deeper into the forest, following the path we ran to escape the Demon. The small barn is torn to pieces like a tornado hit it. Tree branches are broken and leaves disturbed. Hearing the snapping of sticks in the distance, we both stop and grip our weapons. We wait to see if it's one of the dead wandering, or something worse.

Through the trees, I can see the larger barn where I hid the bones, then the road beyond. Route 37.

Sparrow starts moving, blade out and wings lifted so they're not dragging in the leaves and creating more noise. A sharp feeling spreads across my shoulders. I never thought I'd miss having wings. Never thought I'd miss carrying their weight. I wipe at the sweat dripping down my neck and notice it's hotter here. Hell has never felt like this before; angsty and chaotic.

The ground rumbles under our feet.

Sparrow glances over his shoulder at me.

My mind races but I push all thoughts aside as I brush leaves aside with my boot. The ground is dry and cracked.

"You shouldn't have come with me," I mutter.

"You really think I'd let you deliver Lucifer's bones on your own? After what happened last time you were here alone? Who know what kind of royal disaster you'd stir up without me here to point it out," Sparrow says, shooting me a glance as he swipes at sweat beading on his forehead.

I huff a breath of laughter despite my annoyance. "That's assuming you survive long enough to make it to the castle."

"I've survived worse," Sparrow grins, his smile faltering when he looks ahead in the distance, a haze trickling down Route 37 like fog rolling in. "Thought I'd rather not push my luck today." His voice sounds far away.

"Do you see something?" I ask.

The ground shakes again.

"There's no earthquakes in these parts," I whisper to myself.

Sparrow sheaths his blade. "If I carry you into the sky, will you fight me?" his voice is suddenly serious.

I move my feet and notice the dry ground splitting apart, leaving a deep crevasse. The earth groans like a giant monster.

"Run!" Sparrow shouts.

The ground splits further. A molten river bubbles to the surface. Shit. I saw this in a movie once. I leap over the growing divide and start running, headed for the road.

"What's happening?" I ask.

"The land is changing into Alastor's Hell. That Demon is all chaos and fire." Sparrow's running next to me. The earth in front of us suddenly splits with vengeance, magma bubbles up and splashes onto nearby trees, setting them on fire.

I stop quick, splay my arms so I don't fall in, my toes on the edge of another split in the earth. Sparrow grabs my upper arm and we jump across together. He tugs me the last bit of distance–without him I would have missed my mark and fallen in.

Lava hits the back of my calf and burns through my jeans. I ignore it. I can only ignore it because the ground opens up and the barn on route 37 begins crumbling into a molten river. A puff of feathers erupts out of the roof as it cracks and breaks into fiery pieces. Two doves fly into the air but the cheeping of a nest echoes. A distraught expression flashes across Sparrow's face.

"Come on," I urge.

"It's not right," he says. "Harming the birds." He glances at me. "You never harmed the birds while you sat on the throne of Hell."

Memories flash to the front of my mind, memories of feathers in Sparrow's pockets and songbirds on my balcony. "Never," is all I can say.

"It was one of the reasons I agreed with the truce."

Something catches in my throat. Sparrow and his damn love of birds.

"I thought that was because of Thrush," I say.

"Sure." He shrugs. "But mostly because of the birds."

The ground quakes, the sound earsplitting. Sparrow grabs my hand and we run together. We leap over small rivulets of molten earth. We round giant pools of bubbling lava. Route 37 is in the distance but we are forever too far from it. Every step feels like a march toward something darker, something inevitable.

When we finally breach the canopy of the forest and our boots touch pavement, the quaking grows stronger. The asphalt splits in two, spreading our feet.

"Screw this," Sparrow mutters as he reaches down and hoists me into his arms. "Don't fight me," he warns.

Black wings spread and Sparrow bends his knees just

the slightest before launching us into the air. I wrap my arms around his neck and cross my legs around his waist, not wanting to fall and burn to death in a pool of lava. On the list of dumb ways to die, that sounds like the most awful way to go. So I don't fight him. I hold on tight and watch Route 37 disappear over his shoulder.

Soon I recognize the beating of his wings is in sync with the blood rushing through the thick veins in his neck. My stomach growls for blood. I lick my lips, focusing on his neck.

"Just do it," he says against the wind.

I press my lips together because I left a hell of a lot of pride in that cave and I'm not about to have a day's worth of pent up blood lust hit midflight.

"I'm fine," I say.

Sparrow makes a noise that sounds like frustration.

I twist to focus on the distance and notice the castle in the burning caves. My stomach flip flops with the speed at which he's flying. I close my eyes.

"Don't puke on me," Sparrow says as he shifts, his arms wrap tightly across my back, securing my pack, and then he flies faster than I've ever seen a creature move.

TWELVE

THEN

SHAY STOOD at the crossroads while Nero tipped his head curiously as a familiar face stepped out of the shadows.

Then, more followed.

The wind howled through the barren wasteland as Chel, Klaus, Tukka, and Skeele stood before the Crossroads.

Shay glanced over her shoulder. There was nothing for miles. No one was nearby to see or hear them. She shifted on Nero's back, uneasy as to what the Hellions were doing here, summoning them.

Chel tightened the hood of his cloak, eyes flickering with determination. "This is it. They'll come," he whispered, more to himself than the others.

Klaus stood beside him, stroking his white beard. "Do you think this will work?" His voice was hollow, laced with both hope and skepticism. "It's not like we're asking for a simple favor."

Skeele huffed, shifting his weight, the tension thick in his muscular shoulders. "We have no choice. Meg and my children are in danger. Lucifer's war will consume everything if we don't act. You heard the Deacon who came to us."

Tukka's eyes flickered with cold confidence. "We must endure that when the time comes, we can return to defend the throne. The deal is dangerous, but we'll already be dead. What more do we have to lose?"

Shay slid down from Nero's back and took a few casual steps forward, her toes stopping just before the runes on the ground that drew them. Sand brushed across her face from the night breeze.

"This is unexpected," Shay said, watching the Hellions and reaching out to touch Nero.

Nero moved closer with a whinny of agreement. A feeling of apprehension traveled down the tether that connected them.

"I don't like this," Shay said. "What are you planning?"

Skeele spoke first, "There is a war coming. The throne is at risk. We are here to make a deal."

"Have you informed your Queen?" Shay asked. "Calling on the Crossroads Demon might be a conflict of interest."

"She knows the war is coming," Skeele said. "Now. My deal." His gaze darkened. "Resurrection when the war comes."

Shay's expression twisted in confusion.

"I will die before the war." Skeele motioned to the other

Hellions. "Most here will." He paused. "The deal. My soul to you for resurrection during the war."

Nero made a grumbling noise.

"I don't like this either, boy," Shay whispered as Nero nudged her shoulder.

"When you rise again, you will be bound to us. Your freedom will be... conditional," Shay warned. "And in return, we will ensure you are strong enough to face whatever forces the war throws at Meg."

Skeele nodded sternly.

"Can you be sure this is what you want?" Shay asked.

Skeele moved closer. "The Deacons warned me."

"You can't trust them," Shay said.

Skeele held up a finger to pause her. "This isn't the Earthen plane, Shay," he reminded her. "This is Hell. We are not humans. You are barely human. *Trust* only goes so far here."

Shay nodded in understanding, but that understanding didn't help ease the tightening pull in her stomach as she thought of the future that might await her friend. Shay never envied Meg's place in Hell. Throughout the years she'd witnessed more danger threaten the Queen than she'd like to admit. The Hellions kept most of it at bay. Shay glanced between the warriors on the other side of the Crossroads Demon summoning runes. If they'd brought her here for a deal like this—death and resurrection for a future war— she couldn't deny them. Shay sighed internally.

"The deal," Skeele urged. "The Queen's bed is cold and she will come looking for me soon. My soul to you for resurrection during the war."

Shay's eyes flashed red. The tether that connected her to

Nero went taut. The words that came out of her mouth were not of her own volition. They were compelled by the curse of the Crossroads Demon and Nero. "Out of the eater will come something to eat. And out of the strong will come something sweet."

Shay smiled and held out a dusky hand that was unfamiliar to her, one with long necrotic fingernails and a transparent golden ring on her middle finger. After all these years she still looked upon her hand as though it were foreign.

Skeele's eyes widened as he observed the change in Shay. He reached forward and grasped her dusky hand. They shook.

Nero whinnied softly.

Klaus came next. The same deal.

Then Tukka.

Chel was last.

"I can't," Shay's voice didn't match her current half-Demon form. Too much of her humanity was charging through, trying to stop something that could turn completely wrong. It could all go sideways. She'd seen it before. A deal didn't always work out as planned. The Deacons could be wrong. Something could change.

"Focus," Skeele warned. "Too much rests on this moment."

Chel had always been like a big brother to Shay. He protected her during the early days in Hell. Trained her. Forced Jed to buck up and face his feelings. Helped lead the rescue after Alastor kidnapped her...

Shay shook her head and pushed down the unease gathering in her chest. The ice that was flooding her veins threatened to take over. Chel should have a longer life than this; she shouldn't be outliving him, not on any realm.

A sharp tear gathered in the corner of her eye as Chel held out his large hand.

"My deal," Chel said, a smirk tugging on his lips. "I can still annoy you–"

"There is nothing funny about this," Shay warned, sensing something inappropriate about to exit his mouth.

Chel's head tipped in respect. "The deal. Resurrection after death. For the war."

Shay smiled sadly and held out her dusky hand. "Out of the eater will come something to eat. And out of the strong will come something sweet."

Nero whinnied in agreement with the pact.

They shook.

Chel kicked the runes and tugged Shay into his arms. She changed forms, turning much smaller and more human, barely visible within the tight embrace of his large Hellion arms.

"Can't have Jed seeing I made you cry," Chel muttered as he reached down, gently smoothing Shay's disheveled blue hair. His voice held its usual roughness, but there was something softer beneath it, something protective. He took a step back, narrowing his eyes as he tried to read her face, but the faint shimmer of tears in her eyes gave her away.

Shay bit her lip, her expression crumbling, and Chel quickly added, "That half-breed abomination will set my ass on fire if he thinks I upset you." He shook his head, a crooked smile tugging at the corner of his mouth, though the humor didn't quite reach his eyes.

Shay nodded, letting out a deep sigh. "I don't want you

to die," she whispered, her voice trembling with the fear she was trying so hard to keep hidden. The weight of everything that lay ahead pressed down on her, making her feel smaller, fragile. It all felt so wrong. So far from that Montana ranch. A different world.

"You're one of my best friends," she said.

Chel's expression faltered for a brief moment, something unspoken flickering in his eyes. "We can't all live forever, Shay-baby." Chel's words were low, barely above a murmur, almost as if he didn't want the words to leave his lips. He cast a quick glance around, making sure none of the other Hellion guards were in earshot. He had a reputation to maintain, after all; he didn't want the rest of the Hellion guard knowing he might have a heart concealed deep inside his leathery chest.

Shay knew better.

"You say that like it's okay." Shay's voice broke as she looked up at him, her wide eyes shimmering with tears she refused to let fall. "But it's not. It's not fair."

Chel sighed and pulled her into a quick, firm hug, his chin resting against the top of her head for a second too long. He'd never been good with words–his family history was enough to prove that–but the embrace, fleeting as it was, spoke volumes. "Nothing down here is fair," he muttered into her blue hair. "You know that. This is Hell. We are all damned. Nothing is promised."

Shay clenched fists against his chest, holding on just a little tighter. "But this is different, Chel. I need you here. We all do. Meg does. Her children. We need all of you."

Chel stepped back, breaking the connection, and putting a few feet of space between them, his gaze hardening once more. "You'll be alright," he said, as if it were a simple truth. But even as he said it his eyes flicked away, betraying the weight of his own uncertainty. "Hell, Meg'll be alright. She's stronger than you think. You don't give her enough credit."

Shay wiped at her eyes, her breath shaky but steadier than before. "And what about you?" she asked, her voice barely above a whisper. "Who's going to make sure you're alright?"

Chel's lips twisted into a half-smile, one that didn't reach his eyes. "Don't you worry about me. I've survived worse." Oh the stories he could tell her growing up in Lucifer's Hell... he didn't though, because Chel knew a creature like Shay needed protecting. She needed the kind of protection his sister never had. And this was his second chance to provide it.

For a moment, Hellscape appeared to still around them, the heavy silence only broken by Nero's huffs and pawing at the ground. The Demon-horse was eager to end this deal. He didn't like the sensation of Shay's despondence shivering down their tether.

"Look, Shay," Chel said, lowering his voice further. "I don't plan on dying today or tomorrow. But if it happens..." He paused, the weight of those words settling between them like an unspoken promise. "If it happens, you remember this: you're stronger than you think, too. Don't waste time cryin' over me."

Shay swallowed hard, nodding even though her heart wasn't ready to accept it. "I'll try," she said, her voice small but determined. "But I can't make any promises."

Chel's eyes softened for just a second, a rare glimpse at

the man beneath the Hellion armor. "That's good enough for me, Shay-baby. Now wipe those tears before someone sees you and thinks I went soft."

"It's too late," Shay warned. "We've all seen you with Rue."

Chel gave her a small, encouraging nudge before turning and walking away.

Shay watched the Hellions go, a strange mixture of sadness and strength settling into her chest. Nero nudged her shoulder and whinnied a noise of comfort. Shay turned and wrapped her arms around Nero's neck.

"Something bad is coming, boy," Shay whispered. "And I fear we will be caught in the middle."

Nero nodded his head faintly in agreement. The memories of the Fast-Zombie War had not escaped either of them. Years might have passed but the memories were still on their periphery. The death of her parents, the destruction of the ranch, the battle with Clyburn that would forever change their lives.

Shay stepped away, resting her shoulder against Nero's, relishing in the warmth of his body, the steady breaths that echoed across the desert wasteland where the Hellions had summoned them.

"We gotta go." Shay jumped onto Nero's back and clicked her tongue. "Fast," she urged.

Nero didn't need to be asked twice. He took off, his hooves hitting the ground like thunder. Shay's blue hair flowed in the night like hurricane wind, and they found their way back to the castle in the burning caves. They tucked their secrets deep down in their chests, never to speak of them again until the time was right.

Thirteen

Then

Skeele watched Rue and Remington as they sparred
under the fading light of the evening. The clearing around
them was quiet, the rhythmic sound of their blades clashing
and the occasional grunt of exertion echoed. Skeele sat on a
low stone wall nearby, his gaze distant but focused as if
trying to imprint the moment into his memory.

Rue was small but lithe and quick. She moved with the
grace of someone born to wield a weapon, her strikes
precise and measured. She was always underestimated
though, and Skeele took great pride in watching her defeat
the giant Hellions who went easy on her in training.

Remington was taller, his fighting style more deliberate.
The Shadow Heir countered his sister's blows with brute
strength, his jaw clenched in concentration. There was a
natural rhythm to their sparring, a fluidity that came from

years of training together. It was hard not to admire how far they'd come.

Skeele smiled faintly, though the weight in his chest never lifted. Any moment could be his last with them. He knew that as his gaze spanned the edge of the clearing, watching for a walking corpse or other danger. The war was coming and there would be no avoiding it. His fate had already been sealed the moment he'd sworn his loyalty to Meg and the children. Their children. He wouldn't see them as anyone else's. Protecting them was the only thing that mattered now, even if it cost him his life.

Rue lunged forward, her blade narrowly missing Remington's side. She let out a triumphant laugh as he stumbled back, frustration flashing across his face. Skeele's smile deepened, but the shadow of what lay ahead crept into his thoughts again. These small moments, the laughter and teasing, the fierce determination in their eyes, this was what he was fighting for. This was what he'd die for.

"Dad!" Remington called out, snapping Skeele from his thoughts. "Who's winning?"

Skeele chuckled softly, shaking his head. "You're both too stubborn to lose. Just like your mother."

Remington rolled his eyes but grinned, wiping sweat from his brow as Rue smirked. She sheathed her blade with a satisfied flick of her wrist, then plopped down on the grass beside him, catching her breath. Remington followed, collapsing next to her with a heavy sigh.

"You never pick sides," Rue teased, nudging Skeele with her shoulder. "Afraid of hurting our fragile egos?"

Skeele chuckled, an ache behind the sound. "I think I'm more afraid of what happens if I *do*. Besides, the only side I can ever pick is your mother's." He winked and the children groaned and made gagging noises before falling into laughter, their voices cutting through the growing twilight. Skeele's thoughts drifted once more; it was harder to stop thinking of the future with each year they grew. Harder to ignore the omen that the Deacons had delivered to him.

Soon enough, their laughter would be drowned out by the sound of battle. Soon, his sword would be drawn not in practice, but to defend their lives. To defend Meg's life. To die was his duty, and he was just fine with that.

The war was inevitable. He could feel it in his bones, like the chill that set in before a brutal winter. He would fight to protect them even if it meant sacrificing everything.

Rue lay back, staring up at Hellsky, her fingers idly toying with the hilt of her blade. "You've been quiet today," she said, glancing over at Skeele. "Something on your mind?"

Skeele hesitated, then shook his head. "Just... thinking."

"About?" Remington pressed, ever the one to pry. He lacked trust; Meg had instilled that in him. He knew he was a Shadow Heir, he just didn't know of what exactly. He questioned every motive, knew one day it might save his life.

Skeele could have told them. Could have warned them of the darkness coming their way. But what good would it do? They were young, full of life and fire. They didn't need the burden of knowing what awaited them. Not yet.

"About how proud I am of you both," Skeele said instead, his voice steady but soft.

Rue sat up, her brow furrowed in confusion.

Remington's expression turned more serious. "Where's that coming from?"

Skeele smiled again, though this time it was tinged with sadness. "Just... reflecting. You've grown strong. Both of you. And you'll need that strength for what's coming."

Remington exchanged a glance with Rue, sensing the shift in Skeele's tone. "We're ready for whatever comes, Dad. We've trained our whole lives for this."

"I know." Skeele nodded, the words catching in his throat. "But promise me... you'll look out for each other."

Rue's frown deepened. "Of course we will. We always have."

Skeele looked between them, his heart heavy with the knowledge of the omen. He wanted to say more, to tell them how much they meant to him, how he would give everything to save them. How he never expected to have children in his lifetime. But the words stuck, unspoken, as he looked away and rubbed an errant hand over his horns. He realized they'd never asked why *they* didn't have horns or scaled skin.

The sky had darkened, and the air grew colder as night settled in. Tonight he could pretend that they weren't on the brink of something terrible, that there wasn't a future battle waiting to claim them all.

Skeele rose to his feet, his movements slow as he extended a hand to Rue. "Come on. Let's get back inside before your mother starts worrying."

Rue took his hand, rising to her feet with a soft smile. Skeele thought she was lighter than a feather to lift. He shook his head and pushed the thought away. Feathers were not his forte, not his history. And he let the moment of sadness pass knowing that he'd never see them with their wings grown in.

Remington stood and brushed off his pants.

As they walked toward the castle in the burning caves, Skeele lingered just a step behind, eyes scanning for danger in the distance. He wasn't like their father. He wasn't a shadow in their lives, a ghost of what could have been. He would stand with them until the end.

When the time came, he would fall for them. And that, he accepted, would be enough.

Meg's Hell was unlike anything Skeele had ever experienced in his long life. The chaos was mild, the creatures of Hell were not oppressed like during Lucifer's time. He thought of the stories passed between him and the other Hellions. Chel always spoke of how Hell had changed for the better and how he wished his sister could see it. Something pinched in Skeele's chest when he thought of the ways Hell might fall if Meg lost the throne; if he couldn't protect her when the time came. There would be no wildflowers, no songbirds, no freely roaming horse-Demons wandering the royal grounds. No children giggling as they shoved each other during their walk back to the castle, trying to knock each other over.

Skeele sniffed to hide the emotion swelling. He wasn't a creature who should feel these things. Not a creature who should wish for better. Perhaps he'd read too many fairytales. Perhaps Meg had given him too much hope.

FOURTEEN

Now

THE HEAVY, brimstone-laden air pressed down on Meg and Sparrow, a suffocating weight neither of them could shake. Flames flickered from the cracks in the road, illuminating the stone path that wound its way deeper into the royal lands.

The castle loomed ahead of them, a jagged black fortress carved into the very rock of Hell, its spires disappearing into the swirling smoke above.

Sparrow's eyes were sharp, alert, darting from shadow to shadow as they neared the massive iron gates. His hand hovered near his blade and his wings were slightly spread, ready to take to the air if need be. He shot a glance at Meg beside him, her face set in a hard, unyielding mask. She hadn't spoken much during the journey as her mood grew darker with every mile. The tension between them simmered just beneath the surface, unresolved and thick as the ash that floated through the air.

They were both hungry. Moreso each time Sparrow was reminded of the feeling of Meg sucking the Demon poison from his arm.

"Stay close to me," Sparrow murmured, his voice a low rumble.

Meg exhaled a puff of annoyance, her fingers tightening around her blade. She pulled the strap on her bag, tightening it against her back, the bones poking against her spine.

"I'm not helpless," Meg reminded him, an edge to her voice.

"Not what I meant." Sparrow's gaze softened for a moment, but it quickly returned to the looming thread ahead. He was on edge, unsure of how Alastor would react to them since his last visit didn't go so well.

Sparrow was grateful the Hellions kept their distance. They were watching from afar like guard dogs. He noticed Meg shiver in response to seeing them. Sparrow was reminded of her past fear of the feral type of Hellions, Lucifer's type–they weren't that different from Alastor's Hellions. They'd hurt her. But Sparrow promised he'd die before he let them lay a finger on her.

"Let me lead," Sparrow warned as they reached the door.

"Because I'm your prisoner?"

"Yes."

"You're not going to knock?" Meg asked.

Sparrow paused before pushing the door open and said, "We have an understanding."

The giant wooden door groaned as it was opened, revealing a long, dimly lit hall.

Unease shrouded Meg's body. Once her home, the castle in the burning caves was darker than ever. It felt both abandoned yet occupied with decay. It no longer felt like home but a distant memory. Meg shrugged off the feeling. Before this place, she struggled to find home. She'd find another home, always did. Maybe she'd go back to the Florida panhandle and live at the beach house...

A horrible sound came from the Hellion's lair as they passed the slightly open door.

Meg refused to look inside.

Sparrow led her to the ballroom that Alastor occupied.

"What a pigsty," Meg muttered as she took in the chaos Alastor had created.

Chairs were broken and stacked in towering piles. Debris was strewn everywhere. Their boots crunched glass and a warm breeze blew in from the broken window Sparrow had dove through last time he confronted Alastor. The walls pulsed faintly with an eerie red glow as if the stone itself was alive, breathing in rhythm with the malice that filled this forsaken place.

They were greeted by the distant crackle of fire. A thin line of smoke rose to the ceiling of the ballroom as a pile of furniture burned.

Sparrow's fingers twitched with unease, though he kept his expression neutral. He glanced to the far wall and noticed Meg's wings still hung like a trophy, blood dried in drips down the wall. He hoped Meg didn't notice.

They crossed the room. Sparrow led her on the winding

path that led to the cleared portion of the room Alastor inhabited.

The table was there. The map still spread.

"What the fuck," Meg muttered as she took in the scene before her.

———

Alastor was dripping with water, his lips blue. His burn scars had turned black from the lack of oxygen.

The Demon took deep breaths and pinched his eyes closed.

Find my bones. Find my bones. Find my bones!

Lucifer's voice was like an explosion in his brain. He dunked his head into the water-filled bathtub again and held himself under by sheer will until the voice stopped. And then he stayed a bit longer even though his lungs burned and his head felt dull. He pulled back, his body sliding against the side of the bathtub until his cheek rested on the cool ceramic. He blinked, thought the two shadowed figures in front of him might have been a mirage of sorts. Ghosts. Perhaps Meg's mother had come back to haunt him again. He'd feared her return since the moment he'd sliced her with that iron rod and sent her elsewhere.

He blinked. These weren't ghosts.

"Well, well, well," Alastor purred then coughed until he couldn't catch his breath. He leaned forward, spitting water. He stood and pain flooded his body. "I was beginning to wonder if you'd gotten lost. But here you are." His gaze flicked to Meg. "And I trust you've brough the bones? Finally."

Sparrow nudged Meg and a look passed between them.

Meg stepped forward, keeping her eyes on Alastor's face. She pulled the bag from her shoulders and it felt heavier than ever in her grip. She opened the zippered pocket and pulled out the dusty bag from inside. She shook it until the hollow knocking of bones echoed through the trashed ballroom like the sound of wooden windchimes.

Sparrow moved to her side, his body rigid, ready for any sign of treachery. He trusted Alastor less than as far as he could throw him. In this place, the shadows were as much a weapon as any blade. Sparrow had seen the things Alastor could pull up from under his feet.

Alastor moved forward, patting the fingerbone in his shirt pocket as he walked.

"Well done," he said softly, his voice dripping with satisfaction. "You've both done exceptionally well. How did you get your prisoner to break?" Alastor asked as his eyes roamed over her body. He licked his lips. "I could take her off your hands. I know some Demons who would pay well for access to her within the skin trades."

Meg stiffened.

Sparrow's hand edged closer to his weapon.

Neither answered. Sparrow prayed that Meg would keep her mouth shut.

Alastor glanced at the pack on the floor. He kicked it and heard a hollow knocking of dried bones.

Do it. Do it. Do it! Lucifer shouted in Alastor's mind.

Alastor rubbed the single finger bone that was in his shirt pocket.

The Raven King and Meg were watching, expectantly.

"End this," Sparrow urged. "Go back to your life."

"You've taken my throne," Alastor sneered. His eyes were bloodshot.

"You never wanted it," Sparrow reminded him.

"I will take something from you," Alastor threatened. "You've meddled in my trades business."

"Watch yourself, Demon. Without the throne you are nothing but a skin and soul trader." Sparrow stepped forward, his expression cold and dangerous. "You got what you wanted. We have a deal."

Alastor glanced at Meg. "You both will pay."

Alastor bent to open the bag containing Lucifer's bones. Dirt spilled out and stained the floor. As he stood, he reached into his pocket and pulled out the finger bone. He glanced at Meg, his lips pressed to a frown, then he dropped the last bone into the pile.

"We are not here to play games," Sparrow warned.

Alastor's grin only widened as he emptied the bones onto the floor then took the small finger bone from his pocket and held it up.

"You've both walked through fire, bled for this." Alastor smirked as he tossed the finger bone into the pile of Lucifer's bones.

Before Meg or Sparrow could react, the shadows in the room shifted. From the darkness, twisted figures emerged—creatures born of Hell's deepest pits. Their eyes glowed with malevolent hunger as they surrounded Meg and Sparrow, claws gleaming, teeth bared.

"Prove yourselves worthy to Lucifer," Alastor said.

"We have a deal," Sparrow interrupted. "You owe me too many souls. Our deal is binding."

The darkness surrounding them went still as Alastor pondered. "If you're dead, I owe nothing."

Sparrow drew his blade and pointed it at Alastor. "I am the Raven King. No one threatens me. Not an Archangel, not Babylon, and definitely not the bastard son of Lucifer. I will skin you where you stand."

Sparrow reached out with his free hand, gripping Meg's wrist and dragging her behind him.

"Send me the souls. Now." Sparrow stood a step forward, ready to gut Alastor where he stood.

"I need more time." Alastor tipped his chin and whispered something that caused Lucifer's bones to begin smoking.

Fifteen

Meg

WELL, that's disappointing.

I've known about Alastor's involvement in the skin trades since he kidnapped Shay. What I didn't know was Sparrow's involvement. I glance between the two men. Alastor is fucked beyond comprehension. Whatever Lucifer is doing to his mind has turned it to Swiss cheese.

I glance at Sparrow. He doesn't look at me and I take the time to examine his hardened expression and realize I have no clue who he is. I have no clue who he ever has been.

The smell of sulfur and decay is suddenly too strong to ignore. The stone walls echo with the hum of dark energy. I glance at Alastor, his figure half-obscured in shadow. He smirks, always too confident, too unbothered. Something feels wrong. A shifting tension thickens the air making my stomach twist with unease.

I turn to Sparrow. His arms are crossed defensively. His

wings look dull in the dim light, feathers trembling with the vibration in the air.

"You're working with him?" I ask, my voice low and laced with disappointment. It's not a question. When I made the connection a few moments ago the realization fell like a stone in my chest.

Sparrow's eyes flicker with darkness but he says nothing, his lips press into a thin line. His silence speaks volumes. He's not denying it.

"Soul trading, Sparrow? You've been dealing with Alastor all this time?" My throat tightens as the truth sinks in.

Sparrow looks away, his jaw clenched, his silence a scream of betrayal.

To think I was stupid enough to start trusting him, to believe him, to believe in all those things he told me...

I PROMISE, you're safe with me. It won't be like before. You've suffered too much." His lips press to the scar over my heart. "I can never say sorry enough for what we've been through."

"WHY?" my voice cracks, anger builds. "After everything, after all we've been through... you're dealing in souls." All these years we tracked Alastor and anticipated an attack, Sparrow was working with him. My heart aches and the old scar throbs. I am reminded of the moment he tried to kill me; the questions he asked before we got to the barn on Route 37.

"There are things I cannot tell you," Sparrow mutters, not meeting my gaze. His wings flutter nervously, brushing against the stone floor. "We can talk about this later."

I've killed people for less betrayal. I killed his father for less. I killed Lucifer for less. The fury bubbles inside me, a raw mixture of hurt and anger boils inside me like molten steel.

Alastor chuckles from the corner of the room. "I told you she wouldn't understand, Raven King."

My gaze snaps to Alastor, my fingers twitching with the desire to reach for my blade and end this game once and for all. But something in the air shifts, a tremor ripples through the stone beneath our feet.

Suddenly, Alastor's smirk falters, his gaze drifting toward the bathtub where the ground begins to crack open. The fissures widen. Dark energy pours from the cracks like smoke, swirling in a suffocating haze.

The bones.

My heart pounds as Lucifer's bones start to move. Clinking and clattering, they begin to reassemble themselves.

Alastor shakes his head like a dog, dark hair flying wild, then he goes still. His eyes finally clear and a smirk lines his face.

"Finally," he says, voice strong. "He's gone. I can think clearly again." His smirk turns darker, more malicious. "Ah, the king returns." He steps back toward the growing rift in the floor. "And you, Meg, should get ready to bow."

"Alastor!" I yell, lunging toward him, but the ground beneath him cracks wide open. Shadows claw up around his ankles, pulling him into the earth. His eyes glint with a wicked amusement as he vanishes into the void, his voice lingering as he disappears, saying, "The souls have been transferred, Raven King."

I glance to Sparrow, dark energy emanating from him, his eyes brighten and widen as though he's received a power surge.

"We need to go," Sparrow says suddenly, his voice strained but urgent. He steps toward me, wings unfurling.

"Don't touch me!" I swat at his hands and step back. Anger flares. "After everything you've done."

"I'm not asking for forgiveness!" Sparrow snaps, grabbing my arm as the ground beneath our feet shakes harder. His grip on my arm is firm, desperate. "I will explain but we have to go. Now!"

I hesitate for a fraction of a second, anger battling the reality of the situation. The air around us crackles with dark energy as Lucifer's skeletal form begins to stir.

I have no choice. If I stay, if we stay, we will be killed—if not worse.

With a final, bitter glance at the bones assembling, I step closer to Sparrow. He wraps his arms around me, pulls me tight against his chest. His wings beat hard, sending a gust of air and debris around us as we lift off the ground.

The room collapses in on itself as Sparrow flies toward the broken windows near the balcony. I go stiff when I notice my wings tacked to the wall like a trophy. That bastard.

The ballroom crumbles under the weight of Lucifer's resurrection. Walls tip in and collapse, leaving a cloud of dust.

We rise above the chaos, the wind whipping at our faces

as Sparrow flies out the broken window and hovers for a moment. I glance to the ruins below. My heart clenches as Sparrow's arm tightens around me. It looks like a bomb blew out the ballroom.

From the rubble, a voice echoes. Rich, deep and filled with malice.

"Meg..." Lucifer. His voice is chilling, sending a shiver down my spine.

Sparrow moves closer and we both see Lucifer watching us from the balcony. He points a bony finger at us.

"Granddaughter!" he shouts across Hellsky. "No hugs? No apology for killing me?" he laughs something maniacal.

The skin hasn't completely formed over his face and it looks like a half-skeleton man is yelling at us.

Unease is an icepick in my spine.

Sparrow's arms tighten around me.

"Go!" I urge Sparrow. "Get us out of here!"

"You cannot run. Not from me!" Lucifer shouts. "You took my throne, now I will take something from you!"

Sparrow flies faster, his wings straining against the howling wind of Hellsky. I wrap my arms around him, feeling the tension in his body, his guilt, his haste.

Lucifer is back and the world has just become a much darker place.

"Where are you taking us?" I ask.

"The closest portal is the Nightjar's pond," he says.

The ground cracks below us. Lucifer's rage is altering the landscape of Hell.

"Hurry," I urge.

They sky darkens and the Nightjar's call echoes. "My baby, I'll keep you safe," she sings into the howling night.

"Hang on," Sparrow says as he tips.

The pond glimmers from between the tree canopies. Steam rises. Ground rumbles.

I'm not the praying type, never have been––always lacked faith in a higher being–but in this moment I pray that he makes it to the pond before the water is gone and we crash into the boiling earth.

Our arms tighten around each other as Sparrow's wings stretch back and he divebombs toward the pond like a Kingfisher.

"Don't let go," he murmurs in my ear.

I close my eyes. His arms are so tight I can barely breath. My arms are so tight I'm ninety-nine percent sure he can't breathe at all.

Cold water hits my head and everything moves in slow motion. I swear I hear Nero's frantic neighing. I open my eyes, open my mouth, and water fills my lungs. Above us is the pond surface, fire erupting like an explosion beyond. Bubbles rise as I try to take a breath.

Sparrow makes a noise that sounds like he's yelling. Then blackness.

Sixteen

"*Speak. Demon horse.*" The white horse bent
to gently lap water from the lake.

The air on the Earthen plane was unnervingly still.
Nero's hooves struck a pile of rocks with a hollow thud as
he walked closer to the white horse, her presence as silent
and unsettling as the world around them. His eyes, dark
and sharp, flicked toward her. Something had changed. He
could feel it. The darkness inside him which he usually asso-
ciated with the Crossroads Demon part of him, felt like it
was ready to burst.

The white horse nodded her head and urged him to
drink. Ice cracking echoed across the Utah abyss.

"*It won't be cold for long,*" she warned.

Nero moved closer and lapped at the cool water,
watching the white horse warily.

"*Cold water helped me learn how to get the words out,*"
she said, watching him closely. "*I'm not sure why.*"

Nero stopped drinking when his tongue was numb. A
million thoughts ran through his mind.

The white horse's silver mane caught the faint sunlight, reflecting something beyond this world. She had been quiet for a few minutes now, her mysterious aura gnawing at Nero's patience. For a creature so calm, so poised, there was an unnerving power within her, one that Nero wasn't used to–one that rivaled his own.

Then, without warning, her voice, smooth and calm, broke the silence.

"*You're quiet, Nero.*" Her words sliced through the air, stopping him from drinking more. "*But you shouldn't be. Speak.*" She urged.

Nero raised his head, noticing that his entire mouth now felt numbed. He opened his mouth, gnashed his teeth, pursed his lips, huffed in annoyance until... "*How?*" came out.

"*Very good,*" the white horse approved. "*How, what? How can I speak or how can I be?*"

"*Speak,*" Nero said.

"*Come.*" She nodded to the frozen plain and waited for him to walk beside her. "*It took me years to recognize that I was something else. Something other. You see... I never died like the other horses did back in those days. I always lived. I always escaped. Always saw a glimmer in the distance and found myself elsewhere.*" She looked at Nero. "*I get the feeling something similar happened to you.*"

"*Yes.*" Nero nodded, his voice sounded jagged and harsh.

"*You can no longer remain silent–*"

The ground beneath them trembled.

The white horse's eyes darkened, and her expression became grave. "*You feel it, don't you?*"

Nero's heart pounded as the earth beneath them shook harder. The wind, once gentle and still and chilled, began to howl violently, whipping through the air like a warm curse. Ice cracked then melted. The once calm skies above them grew dark and twisted, angry clouds swirling and descending toward the earth.

The Earthen plane trembled as a loud ripping sound echoed throughout, like cloth being torn on a nail.

"*The Veil,*" the white horse searched the horizon. "*Lucifer has returned.*"

The ground buckled, splitting open beneath Nero's hooves as the sky raged overhead. He staggered, his legs stretching wide as he struggled to maintain his balance. Lightning cracked across the heavens, illuminating the twisted storm clouds that now loomed ominously above them.

Then they saw it: a rip in reality in the middle of the thawed plain before them. The Earthen plane wavered, heat and fire blew in, the tear widened, and a handful of Demons charged through.

"*The Veil is torn.*" The white horse nodded in the direction of the mountains.

"*It can't be,*" Nero muttered, his voice rough with disbelief.

The white horse turned her gaze toward the chaos, her serene demeanor shattered by the sheer weight of what was happening. "*Lucifer's resurrection has thrown everything into disarray. His return signals the end of peace, the rise of darkness. The balance has shifted drastically.*" The white horse sighed. "*We worked so hard to avoid this.*"

Nero's eyes went wide. "*What are you?*"

The white horse began galloping. *"Come now, Nero, we must get to safety."*

They ran past the lake which began to steam and boil. Past the plains where icy grass melted and turned brown. Past mountains that tremored and rumbled as rock tumbled down from the peak. Screams echoed in the distance.

They paused near an empty road. *"We must find a tear to Heaven. We aren't too late. There's still hope,"* the white horse said, her eyes reflecting the swirling darkness.

Nero looked at her, incredulous. *"Hope? You're seeing what's happening, aren't you? The world is falling apart. Exactly what the Deacon's warned."*

"Yes, they were a great help in keeping the balance. But now we have one last hope. There is something that can stop him. Something that even Lucifer fears."

Nero's ears perked at that. *"What are you talking about?"*

"I am thought to be lost, a treasure to find,
An ancient relic that transcends time.
They search for me where metals gleam,
But I walk the earth, not what I seem.

I am both the key and the guide." The white horse paused, her eyes distant as if searching through the vastness of memory.

"Where is it?" Nero asked.

"Hidden. Forgotten by most, but it exists. And we must find it if we're to stop him."

The earth rumbled again, louder this time, splitting the ground beneath them. Nero's hooves dug into the dirt, steadying himself as the world continued to crack and break around them. The storm raged and Demons roared as they poured out of the split in the Veil between realms.

The white horse turned toward him, her gaze fierce and resolute. "*It is more than an artifact. It is a key, a weapon, forged to contain darkness itself. But it cannot be wielded by just anyone. Only those who carry both light and shadow can unlock its power.*"

Nero's breath caught and he stared at the white horse, realizing what she meant. "*Meg,*" he whispered, the truth sinking in. "*You're talking about Meg.*"

"*Yes,*" she stepped closer, her silver mane brushing against his side. "*She is half-darkness and half-light. The key to saving this world lies within her.*"

The storm roared louder, the wind tearing at their manes as the earth buckled once more.

"*And the relic?*" Nero asked.

"*There is only one remaining. Hidden somewhere. We must find it and bring it to Meg before it's too late.*" The white horse whinnied and nodded toward a spec of light breaking through in the distance. "*There, a break. Run fast before it closes.*"

Both horses took off, faster than lighting, faster than a black hole, faster than anything. Nothing had ever kept up with Nero's speed, not until this moment. Nero's heart beat kicked up a notch and he tipped his head down, running faster, challenging her. The white horse kept up, gallop for gallop, hoofprint for hoofprint. They stayed side by side. Black and white. If anyone could see them, they wouldn't believe it.

They leapt through the small tear and landed on the

edges of Babylon. Nero paced, shaking off the adrenaline of the run.

Suddenly, his blood went cold. A scream traveled down the tether that connected his soul to Shay's. Nero took off in the direction of the Raven King's lands.

He didn't wait to discuss with the white horse, the pace of his gallop pushed his muscles to the brink. All he could think of was Shay and the terror coming from her.

I'm coming. I'm coming. I'm coming. He chanted, trying to send the message to her.

He leapt over the barrier to the Raven King's lands.

Seventeen

"Shay?" Rue was searching under the couch cushions.

"Yea?" Shay set down her book and watched the girl.

"Have you seen Lucipurr?" Rue kneeled on the floor to look under the couch. "I haven't seen him in a few hours."

"I'm sure he's fine. Kittens like to hide for their naps." Shay stood. "I'll help you find him. Where did you see him last?"

"He was in my room."

A small meow came from the front of the house.

"Did he go outside?" Shay asked, walking toward the door.

Rue followed. "He's never been outside without me."

"Maybe he was exploring. Kittens do that sometimes. He's a curious little thing." Shay reached for the door and opened it. "I had a barn cat as a kid and always found it sleeping in the strangest places. The chicken coop, under the porch stairs."

A man in a black suit was standing on the porch,

holding Rue's kitten. For a second Shay's breath stopped thinking it was Alastor come back to haunt her. She blinked and realized it wasn't him. He was handsome yet... a shadow shifted across his face, darkening his features. Shay thought he might have been another Angel, but the scar on her thigh ached with familiarity. No, not an Angel. This man was something not of this realm.

He stepped down and back until his feet hit dirt.

A twitch of alarm hit Shay. "Who are you?" she asked.

"That's no way to treat a guest." The man stroked Lucipurr's head, his firm pets stretching the kitten's eyelids back.

"Stop," Shay said, reaching forward. "You're hurting him. Give him back to me." She grasped air, reaching for the kitten.

Something like fire and possession flashed in the man's eyes. He threw the kitten at Shay and reached forward, grabbing Rue's wrist.

The ground opened under his feet and in a split second, both the man in the suit and Rue disappeared into the ground. The only thing left in their place was a mound of dark dirt.

"No!" Shay screamed, dropped the kitten, and started clawing at the dirt. "Help!" Shay shouted as terror tore through her, dirt and rocks shredding her fingertips as she dug with her hands.

Nero was the first to arrive in a flash of black, a shadow zooming across the lawn. He whinnied a worried sound.

"Someone took Rue," Shay told Nero, the words came out like a scream. "Some man was here... he had to be a Demon. How did a Demon get here? They aren't supposed to find this place. They aren't supposed to be able to cross into this realm."

Jed was running toward her, Remington and Thrush not far behind.

Shay was still digging. Nero started pacing, he wanted to find the break in the Veil and go after whoever had taken Rue.

He whinnied and relayed the message down the tether that connected them. "Go!" Shay said, "Go find her. Please find her. Oh, God." Shay was trembling with fear as memories of her time in Alastor's hovel flooded her. She couldn't imagine a child with one of those skin trader Demons. "We have to find her!" Shay screamed.

Nero ran toward Babylon. The girl was too innocent to be in the hands of a Demon or worse, Lucifer. He leapt over the stone boundary that surrounded the Raven King's lands. He ran into the center of Babylon, not caring if anyone saw him and he leapt into the fountain.

EIGHTEEN

MEG

I COUGH, light blasting my vision. Sitting up, I gasp in a deep breath then spit out a mouthful of water. The shimmer of the Babylon fountain ripples as I stand. The air surrounding me seems to hum with warmth but the subtle peace is fleeting.

The moment Sparrow tugs me out of the fountain and my boots touch the stone walkway I hear it, echoing throughout Babylon, coming from the kingdom in the distance. A faint, heart-wrenching sound carried on the breeze. My heart drops, the sound unmistakable, and my pulse quickens. Screaming.

"Sparrow." My voice doesn't sound right.

"We need to go," Sparrow says, his body vibrating with alarm. His wings unfurl and shake away the water before he grabs me and shoots forward. He races toward the noise. The closer we get, the sharper the screams become, cutting through the otherwise perfect stillness of Heaven like a jagged blade.

It's Shay's voice.

Something is wrong, very wrong. The type of wrong that buries itself in your gut and gnaws at you, urging you to move faster, to forego thought and only act.

From the corner of my eye, I catch a flash of movement. A blur of black and white. Two powerful forms moving with grace across Babylon. One leaps over the boundary to Sparrow's kingdom.

It's Nero. And... a white horse.

The screaming grows louder as we approach. My stomach twists with every single one of Sparrow's wing beats. I see the house in the distance. People are running. Something is wrong and it feels like a shadow is creeping over everything.

Shay is screaming and digging in the dirt with her hands like a crazy person. Her voice sends a cold spike of fear down my spine.

Sparrow lands, nearly dropping me, our feet skidding against the ground. The moment my feet touch grass, I feel it. Darkness. A flicker of Hell's influence coming from the hole Shay is digging.

Without another word, I push forward, Sparrow at my side, both of us racing toward the commotion.

Shay looks up and notices us. She's covered in dirt and tears drip down her cheeks. Everyone is shouting.

"What happened?" Sparrow roars over the voices.

Everyone goes still. There's a kind of fear in the air I've never felt before. They're all standing stone still, afraid.

Shay, Jed, Nightingale, Noah, Chel, Thrush, Remington, and a soft meow from Lucipurr.

Shay stands, her hands bloody and dirty. "I don't know how it happened, Meg." She hiccups. "One minute we were looking for the Lucipurr, the next he was there. He just... he had the kitten and he was squeezing Lucipurr's head... and he... he threw the kitten at me. Then he... oh God, no..."

"What happened?"

"He took Rue," Remington says.

"Who?" I ask. "Who took her?" my heart starts beating too fast, the hairs on my scalp tingling. "Who was it?"

Shay is shaking her head. "A Demon in a suit. I've never seen him before. How did it get in? How?" Shay screams the question. "How can a Demon breach the Seven Kingdoms of Heaven?"

"Lucifer has been resurrected," Sparrow says.

"Where did he take Rue?" I ask, feeling like I'm losing it. My skin feels like ice, my blood like lava. "Where is she?"

Silence.

Shay looks terrified.

"I want her back!" I scream. "This wasn't supposed to happen!" I have never felt weaker, I have no wings, no ability to *poof*... I glance at Sparrow. I could drain him dry, it would make me strong. His blood would make me fast. I could take from him to find her. I glance at Remm and Thrush. When Nightingale and Noah arrive they pull the boys back, protecting them... from me.

"Stop," he warns. "We get her back together. If you kill me, we lose." He shakes his head. "Stop thinking about it."

Tears cloud my vision. "What do you expect me to do? I will kill every soul in Heaven and Hell and the Earthen plane to get her back. This was not supposed to happen. I was supposed to keep her safe!" Something dark is threatening to take me over. Black swirls in my periphery.

"Mom," Remington interrupts. "Rue is strong. She can hold her own until we find her."

"She's gone." The words hang in the air, heavy, suffocating, as if the weight was going to crush my lungs and choke the life out of me. I can't breathe. The ground tilts beneath me, the walls closing in, my mind spins out of control. Rue. My daughter. Taken. Just like... Elyse. My daughter. Dead. This is nothing but a family curse. All my daughters die. Not her. This ends now.

"No," I gasp, my voice barely recognizable, more of a rasp than words. "No, no, no!"

I stumble backward, my back hitting Sparrow's chest. My knees buckle, my chest heaving as a wave of panic surges through me. Raw, burning heat claws at my throat and my vision blurs with a mix of tears and rage.

"They took her!" The scream rips from my throat, ragged and desperate. My hands fist in my hair, pulling hard enough to sting, but it doesn't stop the spiral of terror. "I should've been here. I should've protected her. Lucifer's bones meant *nothing*! I should have burned them. You're all wrong. You've always been wrong. Handing over his bones was not what I should have done."

I can't think. My mind is a whirlwind of images; Rue laughing, Rue calling my name, Rue's face twisting in fear as a Demon drags her away. I need to find her. Now. I need to...

"They're going to kill her!" I shriek, my voice cracking. "They're going to kill my daughter!" Memories flash faster across my vision... falling down stairs, blood, Hellions, a snowy owl, a jar full of feathers...

I feel like I'm spinning, the world tilting on its axis. I have to get to her. I have to tear down every Demon, every barrier between me and her. I turn, stumbling to my feet, looking for something, anything to help me. My vision is blurry with panic.

I feel Sparrow's hands trying to steady me–someone speaking my name–but I barely hear their words. All I can hear is Rue's voice calling out for me, needing me. And I wasn't here.

"No!" I thrash, pulling away from Sparrow as he tries to hold me, my body lurching forward as I stumble and grab my blade from the holster on my thigh. "Let me go! I have to find her!"

"Meg, stop!" The voice is too distant, too far away to matter.

Another scream rips from my throat. "I can't–she's alone–"

Suddenly, I feel a strange pressure, a subtle warmth against the back of my head. Something soft but forceful, a whisper of magic winding its way through my skull until a blue light clouds my vision. It's calming, soft. I stagger, my breath catching as a thick fog begins to wrap itself around my thoughts. My knees buckle and the house in front of me sways. What is this? I've never felt anything like this before. I knew the rage, the sadness from a few minutes ago. Not this...

"Jed?" his name tumbles from my lips and whispers across my ears. The panic fades, dulled by creeping magic. It wraps me in a gentle, inescapable haze. There's no fighting it.

"Be still," Sparrow whispers in my ear as he lifts me.

I barely raise a finger to point at Jed. I'm gonna get him back. His hand swipes through messy hair and Shay gives a nervous glance. But then, everything goes dark. My body sags, I stumble back into Sparrow's arms.

NINETEEN

MEG

"I'M GONNA KILL JED," I mutter as Sparrow tightens his grip on me.

Whatever spell he used didn't last long. I glance to the side and recognize the inside of Sparrow's house.

"Put me down," I say.

"No," Sparrow replies.

I struggle and kick.

"Stop it." Sparrow shoves open the bedroom door with his shoulder. He drops me to my feet and slams the door closed, backing against it, blocking my exit.

"Get out of my way." I stumble, feeling woozy. I shove at his big body, trying to get him to move.

"Calm down, Meg," he says.

"Move!" I shout.

"You want to be mad? Then be mad. Take it out on me." Sparrow drops to a knee so he's below me. "I can take it. We need Jed. We need all of them to win this." He takes my hand and presses it to his neck. "Do it. I deserve it. Of all people. You can take your anger out on me."

I want to hurt him. I want to bite him. I want to tear him apart. But... the room starts spinning and my heart thrums against my ribcage.

Sparrow stands and I back away, still gripping his neck. My stomach flips in dread.

"You want to use your teeth?" He crowds me until the back of my legs hit the mattress. He pulls the collar of his shirt down. "You can do it. A hundred times if that's what it takes to sate your anger."

"They took my child." I grip his neck harder and swallow down the thickness gathering in my throat.

"They took my child," he says.

"This is different."

"I won't argue that." He nods before pushing me onto the bed. "You are a shade of moonlight. You need to eat and regain your strength. Because the next time your feet hit that floor, we'll be running into a war. And I'll be damned to lose you again."

I flash my teeth, pull him close and sink my teeth into his wrist, tears spilling from my eyes.

Something like fire rolls through my body and he senses it. He tugs at my shirt and I work the buckle of his pants.

Soon we are both breathing heavy, aching, distraught, trying our best to fill a void that cannot be explained.

TWENTY

It was only moments after Sparrow had gotten Meg finally settled in bed, asleep, when the alert came through that the Archangels were at the gates to his kingdom.

Sparrow left the house and flew to meet them. Six Archangels in flowing robes were clustered near the gate.

"What has happened?" Gabriel asked.

"Did she deliver the bones?" Raphael's voice was hurried.

Michael was pacing and rubbing his chest, looking curiously past the barrier into the Raven King's lands. "There are creatures in there..." he seemed worried.

Sparrow smirked at the Archangel Michael, knowing he'd have the sense of kin being close. Jed was in there. Michael's bastard, half-breed son. Sparrow glanced at Raphael and wondered if the Archangel had the same feeling in his chest when he'd been near Demore. Sparrow only recognized the feeling after Meg had told him the truth about Rue and Remington and he'd made the connection.

"A demon broke through the Veil. It took the girl," Sparrow said, staring at Gabriel.

"Meg's daughter," Gabriel paled. "Not again." Rough hands tore through his hair before smoothing his beard. "Christ almighty. *Not again.*"

"They can get in," Uriel paled before blessing himself. His fingers trembled as he kissed a prayer against his hands. "It's all coming true."

The tension among them thickened. Gabriel's eyes flicked to Sparrow, desperation seeping into his expression. "You must return to Hell. You must find her. Now. Lucifer is growing stronger by the hour."

Raphael stepped forward, his eyes gleaming with urgency. "If Lucifer regains full control, the realms will fall into absolute chaos. You cannot wait any longer."

Michael had stopped pacing, his fists clenched. "The longer we wait, the worse it gets. We need *you* to act." His words were sharp, almost accusatory, as if Sparrow was deliberately wasting time.

Sparrow's jaw tightened. He knew what they expected of him. In fact, he knew more than most of them thought. His gaze drifted to Gabriel. Meg's father knew and was keeping secrets of his own. They saw him as the Raven King, the bridge between Heaven and Hell, the one who could stand with Meg against Lucifer's madness. But none of them knew the truth about the children. None of them understood why his every instinct screamed to stay, to protect what was his.

"The girl is my daughter," Sparrow cut in, his eyes hard as he stared at the Archangels. "There's a boy, too. A shadow heir that Meg has kept hidden."

Shock rippled through the group. Even Michael stopped, his eyes widening slightly. Gabriel was the first to recover, his voice low. "Your children?"

Sparrow nodded. "Meg kept them a secret, said they were the Hellion's." He glanced to Gabriel. "She's kept you away for a reason. A good reason."

Voices chattered as the Archangels discussed the new information and how it would affect the coming war.

Wars. Blood and death. Good and evil. A dead Sparrow. A motherless child and a fatherless child. Light and dark. The Earthen plane and the ethereal realms. A burst of bright light. An explosion. Fear and pain. Emptiness.

Raphael spoke softly, almost cautiously. "We didn't know..."

"Of course *you* didn't," Sparrow snapped, the words like ice. He took a breath, rage swirling. "But now you do."

Michael's voice cut through the silence, cold and matter-of-fact. "Every moment you wait, Lucifer grows more powerful. If you don't stop him now, there won't be anything left to protect."

Sparrow's wings twitched in irritation. "I understand the stakes."

Gabriel's eyes softened as understanding flashing across his face. "You are not your father, Sparrow. And you're not alone in this."

Sparrow's jaw tightened. "I know. But this is different. There is too much to lose. More than I ever imagined."

Gabriel nodded and pressed his lips together. He didn't need to say more because this was his family also, a family he wasn't sure he'd ever see again nor have a relationship with if darkness won.

"You'll take half of my legion," Gabriel said.

There was silence.

Gabriel turned to the others. "Hand them over," he commanded.

The others hesitated. Sparrow and Gabriel's kingdoms were the largest, the strongest. The other Archangels, while high on self-importance, couldn't match.

"Our kingdoms will fall," Michael finally said.

"Then so be it," Gabriel barked back. "You've taken enough from others. Taken from my family. Threatened my daughter for years. Imprisoned me on bad intel. Ignored omens you'd known about for ages. Even misinterpreted them." Gabriel's teeth were clenched as he took a rage-filled breath. "I have not forgotten whom you blamed for the Fast-Zombie war. I have not forgotten whom you locked in a cage. Hand over the troops."

TWENTY-ONE

THE AIR IN THE DIMLY LIT LIVING ROOM WAS thick with tension. The walls seemed to close in as the group gathered, the flickering lights casting long shadows on their faces. Rue's absence weighed heavily on all of them.

"We need to move soon," Jed growled, pacing the room, his eyes darting to the map laid out before them. "If we wait any longer, who knows what that Demon bastard will do to her."

Remington, leaning against the wall, watched Jed with quiet understanding. "We'll get her back," he said calmly, though his voice was firm. "But we need to be smart about this."

Chel, arms crossed over his broad chest nodded. "Agreed. Rushing in could get Rue killed. Could get us all killed." His dark eyes shifted between the others. "We have to consider everything. These are no longer the Demons of Meg's rule. Everything will be different."

Sparrow stood by the doorway, his wings twitching slightly with nervous energy. He hadn't spoken much since the planning began, but his eyes were sharp, listening to every word. Thrush sat next to him, idly sharpening a blade, the steady rhythm of metal against stone the only sound for a moment.

"The landscape has changed. Lucifer tore apart the Hell you all once knew." Sparrow described the cracks in the land, the flowing lava, the shifting landscape.

"What about the black mansion?" Shay asked. "The hovels in the forests?"

Sparrow shook his head. "We weren't near those areas. But those Demons have always been sympathizers to Lucifer." Sparrow didn't mention with the transfer of souls and power he'd felt that the Black Mansion and all the Demons involved in the skin trades were more than likely still standing. Hell was greedy with Lucifer at the helm. The creatures would begin harvesting souls from the Earthen plane at a rapid pace for their new King.

Jed stopped pacing and planted his hands on the table, staring at the map. "That reminds me of something. Alastor's blade," he said, his voice low. "The Basilisk blade he used on me... it's unlike anything I've ever encountered. It nearly killed me. That kind of weapon... we need to prepare for it."

Shay, seated at the edge of the room, leaned forward, her brow furrowing. "The Basilisk venom in the blade... it's incredibly potent. If Alastor or another Demon has more of those weapons, we're going to need something to defend ourselves."

"Or better yet, fight back," Remington muttered from his seat next to Chel. His young face was determined, but there was a flicker of uncertainty in his eyes. "We can't go in there unarmed."

Sparrow's wings rustled as he shifted uncomfortably. He cleared his throat, drawing their attention. "I might know where we can get weapons like that," he said, his voice hesitant.

Noah's gaze snapped to Sparrow, eyes narrowing. "What do you mean?" He'd been focused on Thrush, an arm wrapped around Nightingale to settle her nervous energy.

Sparrow rubbed the back of his neck, wings lowering. "There was a Basilisk here once, during the Fast-Zombie War. I had to bury it a long time ago."

There was a beat of uncomfortable silence because most in the room knew what Sparrow did when he returned to his kingdom during that war.

Shay's eyes widened. "You buried a Basilisk?"

"It was already dead," Sparrow quickly added, glancing down the hall where Meg was sleeping.

The room went silent as everyone absorbed Sparrow's words. Thrush stopped sharpening his blade, looking up with a thoughtful expression.

Jed straightened, eyes blazing with intensity. "If we can dig it up, we can make our own weapons. Use the same power that almost killed me and turn it on them."

Chel grunted in approval, his wings flexing. "It's dangerous, but if we can make weapons from the bones and the venom, it might give us the edge we need."

Remington, always ready for a challenge and ready to find his sister, stood up, the fire of determination in his eyes. "So we dig it up, forge the weapons, and get Rue back."

Jed slammed his fist down on the table, his eyes burning with renewed hope. "Then let's move. Every second we waste, Rue slips further out of our reach."

Chel uncrossed his arms, nodding. "We'll need to move fast. We've already lost enough time."

The room was a flurry of movement as everyone sprang into action.

"We don't need to dig it up," Sparrow announced. "I did that a few years ago." He cleared his throat.

"And?" Shay urged.

"I had the bones forged into a supply of weapons. Just in case." He glanced toward the front door. "Some of us have had warning of this war. There have been omens. Whispers. I've been preparing."

"Where are they?" Remington asked. "Did you know they'd take Rue?"

"I didn't." Sparrow pushed away from the wall he was leaning against and nodded toward a blank wall at the center of the house.

Everyone waited, expectantly.

"It's not a true wall," Sparrow said as he crossed the room, ran his fingers across the wood paneling until a faint click was heard. A door opened with a stairwell that went down.

"Hm," Nightingale resounded. "Always wondered if you'd rebuilt father's dungeons."

Sparrow glanced back at Nightingale. "It's not a dungeon. I am *not* our father." He flicked a light switch and began walking down the stairs. "Come on," he called.

They followed him down winding stone stairwell that opened to a large room that was empty except for weapons lining the walls.

"Holy crap," Thrush muttered as he moved toward an array of small blades.

"All this from one Basilisk?" Chel asked, remembering that Meg had sent the mother Basilisk to help clean up the Seven Kingdoms of Heaven. "She was a beast." He admired a long sword with a curved blade.

"Take what you can carry," Sparrow said. "The rest will go to my Legion."

"You're bringing them to Hell?" Nightingale asked.

"Nearly half," Sparrow said. "I can't leave this place empty. I don't know if the Veil will split and reveal the Seven Kingdoms of Heaven for the first time."

Noah made a noise of disagreement.

"If the Seven Kingdoms fall, and we fail, there will be nothing," Sparrow said. "This is not about my kingdom. This is about a safe stronghold against the darkness of Lucifer. There is a reason he was cast out."

There were footsteps on the stairwell and everyone turned as Meg muttered, "Holy fuck."

She was dressed for war. Leathers and holsters, her blade strapped to her thigh. She crossed the room with purpose, stopping in front of a giant blade with a black tip. It was a huge tooth fashioned into a wicked weapon. Meg recognized it instantly.

"Oh momma," Meg whispered. "You made the greatest sacrifice." She reached for what was left of the precious mother basilisk, the one who protected Meg's castle, who protected them during the fast-zombie war, who gave her life to save the Seven Kingdoms of Heaven when the dead breached their portals. It appears she would go on protecting Meg's life and family with her bones.

"Take it," Sparrow urged as he took the opposite tooth. There were two more; one he handed to Remington, the other to Thrush.

Nightingale made a noise.

"They'll go after the boys first," Sparrow said. "Shadow heir," he said softly, pressing the blade into Remington's palm. "If we don't make it, this kingdom falls to you." Sparrow turned to Thrush. "If he doesn't make it, the kingdom falls to you."

Nightingale gasped as Noah pulled her close.

Remington nodded sharply.

Thrush tipped his head in challenge. "Let them try."

Meg moved closer to the son whom she'd done her best to shield and protect and hide. She touched his shoulder, squeezed slightly. "Let's go get your sister. Don't be afraid to let out the *darkness*."

The room was silent as Meg and Remington ran for the stairs. Thrush followed close behind. Then Sparrow. The others ran after them, ready for war.

Twenty-Two

Rue was screaming as she was pulled through the soil into darkness. The Demon was holding her tight like precious cargo. An arm around her shoulders and another around her middle, she couldn't escape even if she tried–even if she wasn't so afraid. She pressed her mouth and eyes closed, petrified of the dirt suffocating her.

Chel would be disappointed that she didn't fight harder but everything happened so fast. One moment she was reaching for Lucipurr, the next that man was pulling her away.

Rue squeezed her eyes closed and tried to hold back the lump in her throat. Her world was spinning. It didn't feel like traveling through a regular portal; being dragged through the ground was something disorienting and violent. Her ears popped, feet hit solid ground, and the arms around her released. Rue fell to a crouch, felt warm stone under her fingertips as she steadied herself. Blinking to force away the feeling of disorientation, she opened her eyes.

There was brimstone in the air, ash filtered through the dim light like dust motes. Rue knew where she was. *Home.* Or what used to be home. The castle in the burning caves felt different. The shadowed corners were darker, more creatures slithering and skittering in the spaces than ever before. She glanced at her feet and wished she'd put boots on that morning. She was only wearing socks, jeans, and a thin shirt.

"Get up." the man in the suit grabbed a fistful of hair and dragged Rue to her feet.

She inhaled a sharp breath and sprung up, the swift movement of her small fist followed her gaze. She almost clocked the Demon in the jaw, but he caught her hand, swallowed up by his much larger one. He twisted her arm behind her back. Rue glared at him. He was definitely a Demon, but more human-looking than any she'd come across before. She glanced across the room. They were in the dining room. There were so many memories of family meals here and she had a feeling the nostalgia for the dining room was about to be ruined.

"I never thought I'd see a Great-Granddaughter," a deep voice echoed.

Rue looked up and up and up. She gulped. She'd never seen a Demon so tall. Never seen horns so large. And if he was calling her Great-Granddaughter, then it could only be Lucifer.

He paced in front of her, hands clasped behind his back as he looked her up and down.

"You're too small," he said as he stopped in front of her. "A runt," he sneered. Lucifer looked disgusted. He paced again before turning to her and crouching. They were eye level now and she couldn't look away from his inky depths. Lucifer reached out and touched her hair, then a fingertip slid across her jaw. "Have you any powers?"

Rue shook her head.

"Can you not speak?" he scoffed, glancing at the Demon who gripped her hair.

The Demon let go and took a step back.

Rue's mouth opened but Lucifer spoke again. "Your mother is much taller. Stronger too." Lucifer took her wrist and stretched her arm out. "Any birthmarks?"

"No," Rue finally spoke but it sounded like a whisper.

"Maybe you're too young. How old are you?" Lucifer asked.

"Fifteen."

"No wings," he frowned.

"No," Rue replied.

He stared, seemed to be pondering her existence. "Your mother was older when her powers formed." He suddenly laughed. "But now she has none. You're both the same. Worthless. Useless. Weak."

Lucifer pressed his finger against Rue's shoulder and shoved. She stumbled back and fell.

Lucifer walked away. He made his way toward a window and gazed outside.

Rue noticed the landscape around the castle had changed; there was no grass or trees, everything was burnt, and rivers of lava flowed through the center of the royal lands where she'd played as a child. A shiver rolled up her spine. The Demon in the suit moved closer to her like he was a guard, like she might escape.

"No power, no wings, puny," Lucifer muttered. "The

Deacons warned that my female bloodline would destroy me." He laughed. "But look at you all, weak or dead. The only one who gave me a struggle was Meg. I will kill her soon enough." He turned to face Rue. "But you... hm. You aren't much..." He squinted. "Your father was a Hellion. That shouldn't make you very dangerous. Your soul is still worth plenty."

Rue nodded, didn't dare tell him the truth.

"Doesn't matter, halflings are just as much trouble." He seemed to be conversing with himself. "It's the ones born half-darkness and half-light that have been the real issue. All the others were easy to kill."

"Her soul has value. We could use her to cultivate the skin trades," the Demon offered. "We lost many willing women during the transition of power."

Lucifer paused. Pondered.

"She looks very human. We could use her to recruit the human women from the Earthen plane," the Demon offered.

Lucifer waved the proposal away. "I will take over all the realms soon enough. The human women won't have a choice."

"Some prefer the willing, your darkness. Some will pay dearly for a willing one." The Demon bowed with the suggestion.

Lucifer growled, annoyed that the Demon dare speak out against his plan.

"Then she is your burden to use as you see fit for the skin trades. But," he raised a long finger. "She will stay here in the dungeons when you are not using her. And then, when I am ready, I will kill her. Just like I arranged for Clea to die, just like I will kill her mother, just like I killed that other halfling that turned into an owl. I will have no bringers of death in this bloodline. I will kill them all," Lucifer promised before disappearing from the room.

Rue shivered as she contemplated the truth she'd just heard; it felt like a thousand pounds of rocks had dropped in her gut. She hadn't seen her grandmother Clea in weeks, last she'd heard her mother said Clea had been sent to the Ether by Alastor. She wondered if her mother knew about the omen Lucifer had just mentioned. She'd learned about plenty of omens the Deacons handed down, most were poorly understood and interference by Archangels and Demons made everything surrounding an omen worse.

"Come with me," the Demon standing near her said. He held out a hand.

Rue stepped back. "Get away from me," she said, glancing around the room, searching for an escape.

Rue's heart pounded in her chest as she stood frozen in the center of the dimly lit room. The flickering light from torches near the fireplace cast eerie shadows against the stone walls, each one shifting, stretching like something alive. Her mind raced, every muscle in her body screamed for her to move, to run, to escape this Hell.

The Demon who'd brought her here was watching, leaning casually against the fireplace, arms crossed over his chest as if he had all the time in the world. He was handsome. Too handsome. With sharp features and dark, unruly hair that framed his face perfectly. His eyes gleamed with something almost playful, a dangerous glint that made Rue's skin crawl then... she shivered hard.

"You don't need to be afraid," he said, his voice smooth,

almost soothing, as if he were trying to coax a frightened animal. "You're not going to be hurt... yet." A faint smirk tugged at the corner of his lips, but there was something dark lurking behind the amusement in his eyes.

"I'm not going anywhere with you," Rue snapped, taking a step back until her back hit the dining room table. The stone floor was warm beneath her feet but that didn't stop the chill from writhing up her spine. She could feel tension tightening in her chest.

The Demon straightened, pushing off the fireplace with an effortless grace that made Rue's pulse quicken. "That's where you're wrong, princess," he said, his tone soft but dangerous. "The dungeon's close. We've been waiting for days. I just thought I'd give you the courtesy of walking there instead of dragging you." His eyes raked over her, lingering, settling on the mess of hair he'd pulled so hard earlier. Rue's stomach twisted with revulsion.

She glanced across the room, desperate to find an exit, a way to escape him. There was a narrow window on the other side of the room, but he was blocking it. She might be able to make it to the door if she could distract him.

"Why are you doing this?" Rue asked, trying to keep her voice steady. "You could have let him kill me and end it all."

The Demon laughed a low, amused sound. "There are secrets I won't spill. Even if you ask nicely." He took a step toward her, slow, deliberate, and Rue's breath hitched. "How cute."

She swallowed, her mind spinning. She needed to do something, anything. Her eyes flicked toward a small table with a heavy, iron candelabra. She knew it was heavy because it fell on Remington's foot when they were nine years old and it broke three of his toes.

Rue jumped up onto the table and rolled across, feet landing hard on the other side, socks sliding as she dove for the candelabra.

The Demon raised an eyebrow, amused. "I wouldn't try that if I were you."

Rue's hand wrapped around the base of the candelabra before he finished speaking. With a cry, she swung it toward him, the heavy iron catching the torchlight as it flew toward his head.

He was fast. Too fast.

Before Rue could blink, the Demon had ducked and surged forward, grabbing her wrist with a grip like iron. The candelabra clattered to the ground with a metallic ring as he twisted her arm behind her back, pulling her flush against him.

"Nice try," he murmured in her ear, his breath warm against her skin. "But you're not getting away that easily."

Rue struggled, thrashing in his grip, but it was like fighting against stone.

"No!" she gasped, twisting as hard as she could. "Let me go!"

She kicked him, trying to break free but he barely flinched, his hold unyielding. The door loomed closer and dread settled in her gut. He was going to take her to the dungeon whether she wanted it or not. And then... bile rose in her throat.

Rue thrashed harder.

"Stop fighting," he said, his voice growing darker, the

amusement fading. "It's over, princess. You belong to us now. Until Lucifer decides to kill you."

Rue's chest tightened with dread as the Demon walked closer to the door, her feet dangling as he held her against his chest with one strong arm across her middle.

The door slammed open. The Demon set Rue on her feet and she made another attempt to flee, rushing to the side and out of their reach.

A giant Hellion stood in the doorway and roared like a boar. "To the dungeons!" The Hellion walked toward Rue–oily skin, horns protruding from its mouth, strange hair like slithering snakes. Rue backstepped, searching for a way to escape the monster. Her mother told stories about the Hellions of Lucifer's time. They looked worse in real life. The Hellion ran at her, grabbing her by the hair. Rue screamed. The Hellion slapped her so hard it knocked her unconscious. Rue's body slumped, nearly lifeless.

———

"ARE YOU STUPID?" the Demon yelled at the Hellion. "Don't damage her."

"She was loud." The Hellion swung Rue's body around like she was a ragdoll, throwing her over his shoulder. "Come with me. I will show you to her cell in the dungeon."

"Let me carry her," the Demon offered, holding his arms out.

"No."

"You will break her. She is tiny. I can't make any money

off her if she'd bruised up and has broken bones." He moved closer. "Give her to me."

The Hellion rolled his eyes before dragging Rue off his shoulder and holding her limp body and with a giant hand wrapped around her waist, he offered her to the Demon in the suit.

The Demon took her, gently draping her over his arms.

"Let's go," the Hellion muttered. "I have shit to do."

The Demon, Dacre, nodded and followed the Hellion to the dungeon.

The Hellion kept glancing back. He was keeping up so Dacre had to assume it was his looks that were making the Hellion suspicious.

Dacre was led down winding stairs. He'd heard about the dungeon here but had never stepped foot in it before. Giant looming shadows shifted behind dungeon windows and doors. Dacre held in a darkness that was swarming in his chest. He wouldn't reveal anything other than stoic strength or risk an attack. Most creatures of Hell didn't understand how he looked so human and most picked fights. He wouldn't risk it here, not with the princess draped across his arms. He tightened his grip on her.

"This one," the Hellion shoved open a dungeon door.

Dacre stepped inside and glanced around the damp chamber. "Get her a cot," he demanded, voice deep.

The Hellion scoffed.

"Do you know how much she is worth?" Dacre asked, glaring. "Lucifer is going to use her to recruit women into the skin trades. She cannot be bruised. She cannot be sleeping on wet stones. She'll wake up with the damp cough and then no one will touch her."

The Hellion grumbled about runes on pale skin and weak children before leaving the chamber and returning a few minutes later with a small cot.

Dacre settled Rue on the bed. "Get out of here," he told the Hellion. "Wait outside."

Dacre inspected Rue's skin for injury; he didn't like the way the Hellion was slinging her around like a ragdoll. The girl exhaled a shallow breath and moaned like she was having a bad dream. She shivered and when the motion didn't stop, he pressed a palm to her bare arm. She was cold. Dacre shrugged off his suitcoat and covered her with it. He watched her sleep, moving the edge of her shirt to the side and read the runes that had been tattooed on her pale skin. Power. Protection. There was something he didn't quite understand, he read the rune a few times and eventually gave up after concluding it had something to do with her aura. He glanced at her dark hair. He hadn't seen an aura in Heaven or Hell but he had heard the stories about the beams of light on the Earthen plane months ago.

"I have shit to do," the Hellion bellowed from outside the door.

Dacre turned away from Rue, reluctantly. He didn't want to leave her here but he would not go against Lucifer's wishes and risk instant death.

"I will return in the morning for her. Lucifer said she is my burden." Dacre grumbled. The daughter of the fallen Queen was going to bring him riches like he'd always imagined. He had family debts to pay off, after all.

TWENTY-THREE

TEARI KNELT ON THE GROUND, HER HANDS DEFTLY adjusting the leather straps of the prosthetic leg she was fitting on the Deacon. Her brow furrowed in concentration.

The Deacon, sitting on a low stool, watched her with grim patience, his eyes flickering occasionally toward Gabriel who stood near the door like a guard.

His back was to them, his tall frame silhouetted against the dim lights of the shelter in the mountain. He was silent, shoulders tense as if bracing for an argument he already knew was coming. Outside, the wind howled through the cracks in the mountain stone, a chilling reminder of the storm gathering on the horizon, of the thinning veil, of the war that would soon tear their world apart. Of dark omens come to a precipice. He thought back to his one love, Clea. They'd started this against Lucifer's wishes. They'd been warned. Gabriel stroked his beard and thought on the omens delivered by Clea. Perhaps he'd interpreted them all wrong and everything he'd done to prevent this war was futile.

"It's time for me to leave this place," the Deacon said, stifling a groan as Teari tightened the prosthetic. "Lucifer has taken over. The Veil is dangerously thin."

Teari didn't look up from her work, but Gabriel's shoulders stiffened at the words. He turned slowly, his expression unreadable. "It's not yet time," Gabriel said firmly, his tone leaving little room for argument.

The Deacon clenched his jaw, frustration simmering beneath a calm exterior. His leg, or what was left of it, twitched involuntarily as Teari fastened the last strap. He flexed the prosthetic experimentally, testing its weight.

"How long?" the Deacon asked, his voice tighter now. "How long am I supposed to wait? Until Meg's fighting him alone? Until it's too late to make a difference?"

Gabriel stepped forward, his face hardening. "We wait until it's necessary, not a moment sooner."

The Deacon looked up at Gabriel, his eyes flashing with defiance. "You do not control me. Every day we wait, Lucifer grows stronger. Every day, Meg gets closer to that fight, and I should be there with her. That is the reason I was saved."

Teari glanced between them, sensing the tension. She tightened the final strap on the prosthetic, made sure the healed skin wasn't pinching, and gently patted the Deacon's knee, signaling her work was done. Rising to her feet, she wiped her hands on her pants, not wanting to get in the middle of the brewing argument.

She knew her place. She was Gabriel's healer and some- times crossed royal lands to assist the Raven King, and sometimes crossed realms to assist Meg. She kept plenty of secrets for all of them, but this information didn't sit right in her gut. Still, she kept her mouth shut.

"When the time is right," Gabriel said, his voice measured and calm. "You can't run in there before all the pieces are in place, it's too much of a risk. You've barely been upright for a few days."

The Deacon stood, testing his balance on the prosthetic. He shifted his weight from side to side. The leather straps stretched, adjusting to his motion. The distraction wasn't enough to cool the fire brewing in his chest. The weight of the Deacon's existence had collected in his body creating an energy so strong it was hard to contain. Now that he was healing, it was only growing stronger. He knew what he needed to do, the urge to cross realms and fight for peace was stronger than ever. He glanced to the Archangel towering over him. Gabriel had always been the most open-minded of the Archangels, the one the Deacons had been watching closely. He was quick to think outside of the box and challenge Babylon. He stood up for what was right, even if it was wrong for the Seven Kingdoms of Heaven. He'd been moved by the peace his last daughter had brought to the realms. Years without war were difficult to come by when good and evil danced the tango under the shadow of the Veil separating realms. A white-flamed ember burned stronger in the Deacon's chest. Gabriel needed a push in the right direction.

"I'm tired of waiting," Deacon muttered, staring at the floor. "It's going to be too late. Much has happened already. You know this." The Deacon's gaze fell upon Gabriel. "You know Lucifer took the girl."

"What girl?" Teari asked, needing to know this instant who it was.

"Meg's daughter," the Deacon said.

Teari froze, knowing that if someone took Rue, Meg would kill them as soon as possible. "You didn't tell me," Teari said as she turned to face Gabriel.

"I shouldn't have told anyone." Gabriel frowned, glancing at the Deacon. "But those damned Archangels will spill the beans faster than a chickadee."

"I was not allowed to live to sit on the sidelines. Not when so much is at stake." The Deacon's leg was trembling.

Gabriel moved closer, his expression softening slightly but there was steel to his voice when he said, "We are all concerned about Lucifer and the thinning Veil. Rushing in alone and without a plan only puts everything at greater risk. What happens if you die before the battle begins?"

The Deacon glared, his jaw tight and fire threading his veins. He was on a precipice. He needed out but he needed strength.

Gabriel's eyes narrowed. "Deacons are quite invincible, but Lucifer will rip you apart if you're not careful, and then what? You think Meg would forgive me for letting you go now, knowing you'd die and never help her? She *doesn't even know you exist*. No one does. As soon as they find out you'll be at risk. Lucifer will slay you in an instant." Gabriel shook a finger at the Deacon. "Soon. Not tonight but soon."

The Deacon fell silent, his chest heaving as anger warred with the bitter truth of Gabriel's words.

Teari, sensing a lull in their arguing, spoke softly. "You're nearly ready, physically. The leg should hold well, you just need to get used to the prosthetic and work the new muscle." She gave him a small nod of assurance, though her eyes held a trace of worry. "But Gabriel's right. You can't do this on your own."

The Deacon's gaze shifted to Teari, then back to Gabriel. Lucifer's power was growing, he could feel it. If he went now, this early, he wouldn't last long.

Gabriel stepped closer. "When the time comes, you go. But until then, you need to be patient. This war will take more than strength. It'll take timing."

The Deacon closed his eyes for a moment, forcing the anger down. It still simmered beneath the surface. He nodded, slowly, reluctantly. "Fine. But when it's time, I won't hesitate."

"I won't stop you," Gabriel said. "I will go with you."

Teari exhaled quietly, relief washing over her. She gave the Deacon a neutral glance before gathering her bag. "Strengthen the leg," she said.

The Deacon nodded, his mind racing.

Gabriel held out a hand, ready to *poof* Teari out of the mountain.

"Healer," the Deacon called.

Teari turned.

"Why did you leave the Legion?" he asked. "You were a warrior once."

Teari glanced at the wall and collected her thoughts. "The true battle is not in taking lives, but in saving them. I seek redemption in healing rather than bloodshed."

The Deacon nodded in approval. "That's what I thought," he whispered.

Gabriel grasped Teari's hand and –*poof*– took her home.

Twenty-Four

THE WHITE HORSE WATCHED NERO GO THROUGH the portal in Babylon. She had a sinking feeling as she thought about what he'd meet on the other side. Portals were no longer a safe bet, especially if Nero was headed to Hell.

She sniffed the air and walked in a circle. From the corner of her eye, she saw Angels watching. She'd been standing in one place for too long. The white horse ran for the nearest tear in the Veil. She could smell it. Fire and brimstone and magma wafted from the cut between realms.

The white horse leapt through the tear, a shiver running down her spine as she anticipated the chaos which would spill over into Heaven soon enough.

She galloped away from the nearby steaming pool of magma. It had been ages since she'd stepped foot in Hell. In the distance, she heard a sharp whinny of distress.

"Nero!" the white horse yelled. She moved in the direction the sound came from and listened again. *"Where are*

you?" Smoke was rising from a crack in the ground and settled like a smog–visibility was low.

The noise echoed again. It sounded like Nero was sputtering or drowning.

The white horse dashed toward his voice; past tall trees, barren land, and cracked roads. The dead wandered close by. She crossed a road and what looked like a dried up stream. Nero's voice was louder now.

He whinnied a panicked sound.

The white horse saw the shimmer of his black coat. She came to a clearing in the forest. She'd been here before but it looked very different now.

A fine mist of rain fell over the once full pond. Now it was nothing more than thick mud. And Nero was stuck.

———

NERO'S HOOVES sank deeper with every desperate lurch. The more he fought, the more the mud gripped him, cold and unyielding, pulling him down. His nostrils flared and he let out a panicked whinny, twisting his head around, searching for any glimmer of hope beyond the misty pond.

The Nightjar fluttered nearby, its shadowy form darting anxiously from side to side. A whisper of cold air brushed over Nero's ear as the spirit coiled near his face, its voice low and hurried.

"He dried up my pond. Stop struggling, Nero! The more you move, the worse it'll be," the Nightjar murmured, its tones urgent yet strangely soothing. She darted down to examine his legs, flickering from one side to the other in restless motion. The Nightjar touched Nero, shoved at his rear, wrapped her arms around his neck and tugged, but she could do little to free Nero from the mud's merciless grasp.

Nero's muscles quivered with the strain, his breathing grew shallow, exhaustion dragged his head lower. He was sinking and could feel the cold seeping into his legs. The weight of the mud anchored him, draining his strength. For a moment he stilled, obeying the Nightjar's advice. Despair clawed at him just like the mud.

Then, from the mist, a soft glow emerged. Slow and steady the light grew brighter, slicing through the gloom, until the slender form of the white horse appeared. Her coat gleamed like starlight, her mane flowed like a river of silver as she approached with calm, deliberate steps.

"Nero," she called softly, her voice a warm contrast to the cold air and biting mud. She stopped a few paces away, assessing the situation with eyes full of patience.

The Nightjar fluttered toward her, casting a relieved shadow across the white horse's face. "He's sinking fast," the spirit whispered, urgency in her voice. "We don't have much time. The muck will swallow him soon."

The white horse nodded. She stepped closer, her hooves somehow gliding lightly over the mud's surface. She nudged Nero's neck, a gentle encouragement, and them positioned herself beside him, muscles tensing with quiet strength.

"I know you're tired, Nero," she murmured. *"We've got to get you out. When I say to move, push up with all the strength you have left. I'll lift as you press."*

Nero, filled with determination, gave a small nod. He braced himself, feeling the warmth of her presence beside him.

"Now!" she commanded.

With a final fierce effort, Nero heaved upward, his hind legs pushing through the thick mud as the white horse lifted him from his side, guiding his weight with surprising force. The Nightjar whispered encouragingly, its voice filling his mind with steady, rhythmic words as he strained forward inch by inch.

At last, with a mighty lurch, Nero stumbled free, his body collapsing onto firm ground. He lay there, panting, the mud clinging to his legs.

He inhaled deep breaths, legs twitching as he realized how close to death he'd just been. Drowning in mud was a fate he wished on no one.

"Gather your strength," the white horse said, taking in their surroundings.

"The dead will come soon," the Nightjar warned.

The white horse nuzzled Nero's shoulder gently. *"Why did you come here?"* she asked.

"A Demon broke through into Heaven. It took Rue." Nero coughed and moved his legs, getting ready to stand again. *"I must find her. She's just a child."*

"I saw a girl..." the Nightjar floated toward the road. She pointed. "A man took her from the castle to the Black Mansion. I followed them."

"Where is she now?" Nero asked, moving to stand.

The Nightjar worried her hands and glanced toward the cabin on the other side of the muddy pond. "Last I saw, he was bringing her back to the castle in the burning caves, she looked asleep in the backseat."

———

THE ENTRANCE to the burning caves loomed before them with the massive castle carved into the mountainside, molten lava now spilling down its craggy surface. Nero paused, his dark eyes narrowing at the sight. The castle's blackened towers twisted toward the sky like claws as flames flickered along the walls, casting an eerie glow on the ancient stone.

Beside Nero, the white horse stood calm but tense, her silver coat gleaming in the dim light. Together they moved forward, silent and alert, their hooves echoing on the rocky path.

Just then, Nero's gaze snapped to a figure approaching the castle gate. A Jeep stopped and a man in a suite got out before opening the back passenger door.

The white horse took a small step forward. *"Is that..."* she whispered, narrowing her eyes on the man in the suite.

A teenage girl jumped down from the passenger side.

"Rue," Nero whispered, nostrils flaring with a surge of protective anger. He took a step forward, muscles bunching, ready to charge, ready to change forms and get her.

The white horse blocked his path with a gentle nudge, her voice low but firm. *"We need to be careful, Nero. That castle is not what you remember."* She motioned to figures in the distance. *"Lucifer's Hellions have noticed us."*

"I don't care," he growled. *"Rue needs us, now."* He tried to push past her, his heart pounding, but the white horse sidestepped, her eyes filled with urgency.

"Nero—look!"

They both turned, and a shiver went down Nero's spine. Emerging from the shadows beyond the gate was a staggering mass of bodies, gaunt and hollow-eyed, each one moving with jerky, unnatural movements. The stench of decay filled the air, and the groans of the undead grew louder as more poured out from the surrounding forest.

Nero pawed the ground, a deep rumble of warning in his throat. *"The dead. Watch out for the fast ones."*

The white horse took a step back, ears flattened as she scanned the horde that stretched in all directions. *"We're outnumbered,"* she said, her voice tense. *"If we charge in now, we'll be torn apart before we can reach Rue."*

Nero's eyes stayed locked on Rue's distant figure as the man in the suite guided her through the castle door. His desperation flared as he looked at the white horse, determination blazing. *"I have to try,"* he said, but the sound of the zombies' footsteps closing in forced him to hesitate.

The white horse's gaze softened. *"There's a time for everything, Nero. Right now, we need to live to fight again. We can go back and tell Meg what we've found."*

The horde pressed closer, hands reaching, mouths open in silent cries. The undead surrounded them on all sides, their skeletal faces twisted in hunger. Nero's heart sank, the bitter taste of frustration mixing with the scent of death around them.

"So many do not belong here." The white horse glanced from face to face. *"The realms are drastically unbalanced."*

With a frustrated snort Nero backed up, and together they turned, galloping away from the swarm of zombies.

They sped up, but... the horde moved fast–faster than before.

"No," Nero whinnied. *"Run!"*

It was too late, the horde was a mix of slow and fast and the horses had waited too long to retreat.

Suddenly, the white horse's eyes went wide with fright. *"Go, Nero,"* she urged. *"Go back. Go back and find the relic!"*

She whinnied in pain as one of the dead scraped her flank.

Nero changed forms, full Demon. He shook his head as he doubled in size, his long black tail and mane became stiff as needles and sharp as razorblades. His veins became giant ropes of obsidian, twining and swirling under his skin like protective armor. Fire was collecting in his throat as another one of the dead scrambled toward the white horse.

"Go," she urged.

"I will not leave you to die," Nero said as he breathed fire and burned the walking dead to cinder.

"Don't waste their souls," the white horse begged. *"They are innocent. Lost. We must defeat Lucifer so they can be set free."*

Nero ignored her and burned the land around her injured body. When he was done, there was only a small white horse surrounded by char for a mile. He delicately picked her up in his mouth, felt the way her body sagged. He ran her back to the Nightjar's cabin, kicked open the door and set her inside.

"Oh, my baby, what have you brought me?" the Nightjar hovered over the injured white horse. "She's so damaged."

The Nightjar wasn't more than an anxious shadow at the moment.

"Watch her for me," Nero said.

The Nightjar's head turned quickly to face him. "You can speak?"

Nero nodded. *"I must find the relic. I will return for her."*

"You must be fast, Nero," the Nightjar said. "Lucifer's Hell is going to kill us all."

"I am thought to be lost, a treasure to find,
An ancient relic that transcends time.
They search for me where metals gleam,
But I walk the earth, not what I seem.

I am both the key and the guide." The white horse was mumbling softly, blood oozing from her wounds.

"What's that, baby?" the Nightjar gently set the doll in her arms down on a nest of leaves and sticks and moved closer. She bent to lean her ear next to the white horse's mouth. "Tell us again."

Nero shifted closer and nudged the white horse with his snout.

She repeated the phrase. Nero whinnied in agitation, language was not his skill, he'd only just learned how to talk. The white horse was speaking in riddles.

"An ancient relic that transcends time," the Nightjar set her ghastly hand on the white horse's head, touched her ear and wiped away a smear of blood. "Why don't you speak plainly and tell him what that is?"

Nero was looking between the two, confused.

"It's a Deacon," the Nightjar finally said.

"The Deacons are all dead," Nero said. *"Alastor killed every single one of them."*

"No," the white horse whispered. *"Gabriel knows."* Her eyes were closing, her muzzle sagged. *"Saw it with my own eyes. On the edge of his lands near the mountain."*

Gabriel. Nero snapped his teeth before glancing at the Nightjar. *"Keep her alive."*

The Nightjar shifted, floated around the white horse and inspected the wounds. "What is she?"

"A horse," Nero said.

"No. No this beauty is much more than a horse. She's already healing. She is so white and pure. Like the heat of the sun." The Nightjar touched the white horse's mane. "You've found a creature some have only ever wished to meet. Look how her hair sparkles. This is a pure soul. Something... *original.*"

"Keep her safe," Nero said before turning.

"Stay out of my pond!" the Nightjar shouted after him. A warning. They had worked too hard pulling him from the mud.

Nero didn't need to be told twice. He'd nearly died in the mud, and he still had it stuck in his ears and hooves, making his black coat look mottled. He would never go near that pond again. Instead, he ran. Faster than lightning. He leapt over pools of magma and deep cracks in the ground until he saw a tear in the Veil. It didn't take long, the Veil was ripping all over. In some places he could clearly see the Earthen plane like a picture between the pines. Demons crawled through. Nero didn't need the Earthen plane. No, he needed the Seven Kingdoms of Heaven. When he finally saw the slice ahead, he leapt through.

———

Nero paced, cooling his hooves on the luscious grass of Heaven. He took in his surroundings, unsure of whose lands he'd came through into. There were Legion Angels in the distance who had noticed him. Nero began running. He didn't have time to fight. He scanned the landscape, recognizing the mountains in the distance that edged Gabriel and the Raven King's lands. He headed in that direction, outpacing the Legion in a heartbeat.

Nero slowed as he got closer to the mountain. He wove between giant oak trees and trotted toward Gabriel's house. But, something caught his eye near the base of the mountain. A figure moved slowly. Wood knocked against stone, leather squealed as it stretched, a man moaned in pain.

The man was muttering, pausing to catch his breath against a tree trunk before glancing up, eyes focused directly on Nero.

Nero couldn't ignore that the air around the man was humming.

It was a Deacon.

"You," the last Deacon said with a smile. "I knew you'd find me." The Deacon waved at the black Demon horse. "Come closer. I am not as nimble as I once was." He motioned to the prosthetic leg.

Nero trotted close to the Deacon then knelt so the man could get on his back.

"Take me to the fallen Queen." The Deacon wrapped his hands in Nero's mane and held on for dear life.

"She has crossed over into Hell," Nero warned. *"I must find the split in the Veil. Don't let go,"* he warned.

The Deacon smiled.

Twenty-Five

Rue had been sitting in the dark for what seemed like hours. She shivered under the blanket and curled into a tighter ball. She was in a crap situation. Rue hoped someone would save her. She understood it had to be a calculated rescue. Her mother and the Raven King were planning on war. They couldn't risk a rescue mission and throw off their plans. Rue thought of her mother; she didn't seem that different without her wings. She still carried herself the same as she always did–tall, chin up, warm only to those closest to her. Rue blinked back the tears, hoped that one day she'd be as strong as her mother was... is. As strong as her mother is.

Rue's stomach growled. It made her think of the kitten and she wondered if Lucipurr was missing her. She hoped someone was feeding him. And cuddling him after the jerk who dragged her into that hole had tossed Lucipurr through the air like a stuffed animal. Rue wanted to go home. She sniffed back tears, noticing the blanket covering her smelled slightly familiar. A little bit like brimstone and pine, like how Hell smelled when her mother was Queen.

The door opened, its hinges squealing and echoing against stone walls. Rue scrambled to the corner of the cot and in the light she noticed she hadn't been covered with a blanket, but a suitcoat. She rubbed a finger over the smooth fabric. Strange.

"Get up." The handsome Demon was back, dressed in black slacks and a black button down with the sleeves rolled up to just below his elbows.

She wasn't prude. She'd read plenty of books and watched plenty of movies. She was a red-blooded teenager and knew a good-looking guy when she saw one. Why he was kidnapping her and then saving her from instant death was Rue's question.

Rue's eyes were wide as she stared at him. "I want to go home. Now."

The Demon chuckled. "Not today."

"My mother will come for me. She will kill you."

The Demon took a calming breath and waved toward the door. "Until she shows, we have things to do today."

Rue stared. The Demon's black hair was tousled, and his sharp features were unnervingly attractive. His dark eyes met hers with an unsettling calmness, betraying nothing of what he might be thinking. Dressed the way he was, he looked out of place in the grim dungeon, like a polished predator in a cage of filth. Rue was suddenly self-conscious.

"Get up," he urged, voice low and smooth but without warmth. "It's time to go."

"No," Rue rasped, fear lacing her voice.

"You're to be presented," Dacre replied, his gaze flicking

over her with a hint of disdain. "The Black Mansion awaits."

Rue's heart sank as she scrambled to her feet. There was a sinking feeling in her gut. Dacre motioned for her to follow, and though her legs were feeling like jelly, she had no choice. She didn't want to be left alone in the dungeon with the door open. She knew the creatures that had been left to rot behind these doors—she'd listened to their guttural cries for hours throughout the night.

Rue followed the Demon down damp hallways dripping with grime and coated in lichen. Oil-like liquid seeped from under doors and down walls. Rue was relieved when they started walking up the winding stairwell and made it to the door to the outside.

The Demon held it open as Rue walked through. There was barely a glow from the sun as the sky was something darker than ochre. Ash filtered through the air, heat wafted off the pools and rivers of magma in the nearby royal grounds.

Rue sucked in a breath of surprise at what her home had become.

There was a black Jeep waiting. Something larger than normal, lifted and with big tires. The Demon opened the back door and motioned for her to get inside. Rue looked up and judged the distance from the ground to the seat.

"Need help?" the Demon asked, a grim expression plastered on his face as though helping her might disgust him.

"No." Rue straightened her shoulders and gripped the doorhandle.

"Might be easier with wings, princess." The Demon mocked.

Rue sprung up, grabbed the "oh-shit" handle over the window and swung her legs inside. She slid onto the seat and refused to look down at the Demon. He slammed the door closed, muttering something in Hellspeak.

Rue soon understood the reason for the giant tires on the Jeep. The road was bumpy, broken and there were deep potholes or sometimes no road at all.

Rue was starting to feel sick with all the jostling. She braced her arms against the door and seat and closed her eyes, holding back bile. She was thankful when the vehicle finally stopped.

Rue glanced out the window. The Black Mansion appeared as dark and foreboding as its name suggested.

The Demon opened her door and held out a palm to help her down.

Rue steadied her hands on the door and seat and jumped, ignoring him. She landed on two feet and then took a step away from the Demon. She smoothed dirty hands over her T-shirt and glanced at her socked feet. The driveway was crushed stone, sharp and glossy. It pressed through her socks threatening to cut her feet.

The Demon took notice and his eyebrow rose in offering to carry her across the sharp stones.

"Don't touch me," Rue warned.

The halls of the Black Mansion were cold and grand, every inch of the place dripping with malevolent elegance. It smelled like freshly cut wood and Rue noticed some rooms were being painted in black and silver. Elaborate wall paper was being hung, embellished with a matte black design. She decided the décor was actually pretty and if she were in a different predicament, she might have enjoyed it.

When they entered the main chamber, Rue's breath hitched. It was filled with Demons, all of them watching her with gleaming, predatory eyes. The room was lit by the eerie glow of fire pits casting flickering shadows on their sharp teeth, horns, and scaled skin. The Demons sat on dark elaborately carved chairs and lounges, like cruel kings.

The handsome Demon stood at her side, his presence both a shield and a threat. He led her toward the center of the room, where all eyes fell upon the small ex-princess with eyes unlike her mother's and long dark hair.

"One moment," the Demon said as he walked out, leaving her alone.

Rue swallowed hard. She glanced around the room searching for a weapon or a way out.

"She doesn't look like much," one Demon sneered, his crimson eyes narrowing as he leaned forward. "So small and fragile."

"No wings. Too human," another added, a smirk tugging at gruesome lips.

Rue went stiff, her heart pounding in her chest. She knew they could sense her fear. They were feeding off it, saying terrible things to make her scared. Rue couldn't slow her heart beat and calm herself.

"She won't last long on the bargaining table," the first Demon laughed. "Too weak."

"Let's see what she's made of," a third Demon growled, stepping forward with a goblet in hand. The liquid inside was thick and red.

"No," Rue whispered, her stomach churning as she recoiled. She didn't drink blood, she was too young to need it.

"Drink," the Demon commanded, his voice a growl of amusement. "It'll make you stronger."

"Rue backed away, but the Demon was too fast. He grabbed her arm and shoved the goblet to her lips. Rue gagged as the metallic taste filled her mouth, the blood spilling down her throat. She choked and sputtered, spraying droplets of blood on the grotesque Demon's face.

The other Demons laughed, taunting. Tears blurred Rue's eyes as she tried to spit out the blood coating her mouth.

"Enough!" The handsome Demon in the suit had returned, his face darkened with fury, fists clenched at his sides. His voice cut through the laughter like a blade.

Dacre remained silent, his expression unreadable. But there was a tension in his body, a flicker of anger in his eyes as he watched them.

The room fell silent as all eyes turned to him. He stepped forward, his cold gaze locking onto the Demon who'd forced the drink on Rue.

"You don't touch what belongs to me," Dacre said, his voice dangerously low.

The offending demon raised an eyebrow, unfazed. "Your little pet?" he mocked. "She's not going to last long anyway. What does it matter?"

Dacre's anger flared but before he could speak, another Demon chuckled from the corner of the room. "He always did have a soft spot for the fragile ones," he said slyly. "Maybe she reminds him of–"

"Shut your mouth," Dacre growled, stepping toward the one in the corner, hands curling into fists.

The Demon's smirk widened. "I wonder if she knows your name yet," he taunted, glancing a Rue. "Has he told you, little lost princess? Does she know who you really are, *Dacre*?"

Rue's head spun as the Demon's words set in. His name; Dacre hadn't wanted her to know. She didn't recognize it or him for that matter.

Dacre's eyes burned with fury, his jaw clenched. He took one menacing step toward the Demon, and for a moment it looked like he would strike. The Demon's eyes went wide and its goblet fell to the floor, staining the tile in thick red blood.

Dacre turned sharply on his heel and grabbed Rue's arm. "Come on," he hissed through clenched teeth.

Rue stumbled after Dacre as he dragged her from the room, her mind reeling. What had that Demon seen on Dacre's face? It was enough to scare him straight. Rue couldn't see a thing with Dacre's back to her. Her short legs were running to keep up with him and her socked feet slid on the smooth, tiled floor.

They went up the stairs to a corridor that was decorated in peach and muted purples. The décor was a stark contrast to downstairs. Dacre's grip on her arm tightened.

When they reached a closed door at the end of the hall, Dacre released her roughly, his back to her as he stood with his hands braced against the wall. His shoulders heaved with barely contained rage.

"What just happened?" Rue demanded, still tasting blood in her mouth. "Why did they say your name like that?"

Dacre didn't turn around. When he spoke, his voice

was cold and distant. "Don't ask questions you're not ready to hear the answers to, little princess."

Rue clenched her fists, anger simmering beneath fear. "What are you going to do to me?"

For a moment, Dacre was silent. Then, without looking at her, he replied, "I'll keep you alive." He knocked on the closed door.

The words weren't a comfort, not from him.

A female Demon opened the door and smiled at Dacre.

"Look what the cat dragged in," the Demon woman crooned. She reached out and drew across Dacre's chest with a red lacquered nail.

Dacre grabbed the woman's hand to stop her. "Not now." He motioned to the girl.

"Lucifer's balls," the Demon woman muttered. "What is that? A child? A human child?" The woman's eyes settled on the blood staining Rue's lips.

"Barely..." Dacre released the woman's hand. "She needs some... assistance." Dacre leaned closer to the beautiful Demon female and whispered something in her ear. The woman nodded, glancing at Rue a few times before she finally said, "I understand." They spoke in hushed Hellspeak for a moment.

Rue leaned closer, trying to eavesdrop. She knew little Hellspeak-only what the Hellions had taught her-but she wasn't fluent. Her mother feared that if she learned the language she might be tempted to run away when she got older and be lost to the realm of Hell. Or at least that's what she'd told Rue over the years.

Dacre stepped away and motioned for Rue to follow the woman. His eyes fell on her lips.

Rue licked them, tasted crusted blood. Her hands touched her face and scraped at the dried blood dripping down her chin.

Dacre frowned, his lips pressed into a thin line. He looked thoroughly pissed.

"Go, Dacre," the Demon woman said, waving him away before turning to Rue. "Come here, little thing." She reached for Rue's hand. "I won't hurt you." She glanced at Rue's socked feet. "We'll get you some shoes and clean clothes. Are you hungry?"

Rue moved so she could look past the doorway. There was an apartment beyond the threshold. It was tastefully decorated and it looked inviting. Warm and... safe.

"Are you hungry?" the woman asked again.

Rue shook her head. "Not anymore."

She frowned. "My name is Kit."

Dacre's footsteps disappeared behind them.

"Please come inside," Kit urged.

Rue was admiring the woman's sharp teeth, red lips, and curly hair when a strange sound echoed up the stairwell.

"Please," Kit reached out. "Now." There was urgency in her voice.

The stairs in the distance groaned as something big ran down them.

A guttural scream ricocheted against the walls. Rue turned, ready to run down the stairs and out the door but Kit grabbed the girl by the back of her dirty shirt, dragged her inside the apartment, slammed the door, and locked it. She pushed a heavy table in front of the door.

"You weren't supposed to hear that," Kit said.

"What was it?" Rue asked.

Kit looked away, ringing her hands. The walls of the mansion shook and something boomed under their feet.

"The bathroom is this way," Kit waved for Rue to follow. "I notice you don't have wings yet." There was concern in her eyes. "You wear a size four? And it looks like size six shoes?"

Rue shrugged. "I'm not sure. I've just always had clothes and shoes that fit."

"Poor princess," Kit frowned.

"Please don't say that to me. I'm not poor. I was kidnapped. Threatened with death and now I'm going to be used by you people." Rue was annoyed and she didn't want pity from anyone, let alone this Demon woman.

"I apologize. I didn't mean it like that." Kit sighed.

Something slammed and the walls of the mansion shook again.

"Hurry. Get washed up. Get that blood off you." Kit led Rue into a tidy bathroom. She opened a cabinet and removed towels, setting them on the counter. "Help yourself to whatever you need. Take your time. I'll find you some clothes."

Kit closed the door and locked it from the outside.

Rue rubbed her arms and looked in the mirror for the first time since the morning she was kidnapped from the Raven King's house. She scrubbed her face, barely believing all that had happened. Her hair was a tangled mess. There was dried blood dripping down her neck and smeared across her cheeks. Something didn't feel right. Her stomach was aching and rolling like she'd eaten something spoiled.

She didn't feel the need to vomit or sit on the toiled. It was almost as if she... wanted more.

Rue turned on the shower and peeled off her filthy clothing. She found pleasantly scented soaps and shampoo. When Rue was done, she was clean but her hair was more tangled than before. Rue wrapped a towel around herself and padded to the sink. She searched the drawers for a comb and heard a knock on the door.

"Can I come in?" Kit's muffled voice asked.

The floor rumbled under Rue's feet. Something was happening downstairs.

The door opened before Rue could answer.

Kit's large eyes looked the girl over. "You're looking better with that blood off your face."

Rue stared. She wasn't sure what to say.

"I found you some clothes. Jeans, a clean shirt, something warm to sleep in." Kit held up a pair of fuzzy slippers. "I don't have any shoes in your size so these will have to do. We'll get you more clothes from the Earthen plane."

"Why bother?" Rue asked.

"Dacre said the dungeon gets cold at night. He doesn't want you to get sick."

"The cold doesn't matter. Lucifer is going to kill me." Rue blinked then looked at her reflection in the mirror. Small fingers tried to detangle her hair as tears dripped down her cheek. "It's only a matter of time."

"Don't dwell on that." Kit shushed. "During Lucifer's reign, death comes for anyone and everyone. And now he's back." Kit picked up the comb. "Get dressed, I'll help you comb out the knots."

———

RUE WAS DRESSED in borrowed clothes and sitting at Kit's kitchenette table, a grilled cheese sandwich in front of her and a Coke in a can. Her toes finally felt warm in the fuzzy slippers.

"Don't waste the food," Kit warned. "Now that Lucifer is back, I don't know when there will be more."

Rue took a small bite as Kit sat behind her, methodically detangling the knots in her long hair.

"Who tattooed those runes?" Kit asked.

Rue pressed her lips together.

"Don't want to tell me?"

"Nope," Rue said.

"Why those runes?" Kit asked.

"I can't remember," Rue lied. She knew exactly why Jed had marked her skin with protective runes and strength spells. Too bad none of them seemed to work because here she was. But she wasn't dead yet, so maybe they did work a little bit.

When Kit was done removing the tangles, she went to the bathroom and came back with hair ties and pins. "Let's braid it to prevent more tangles tonight."

"No one has ever braided my hair before," Rue said, taking a sip of the Coke. She finished her sandwich and sat back. Having grown up in Hell, Rue was comfortable around Demons of all type. Kit was nice and was helping her for the moment. Rue relaxed against the back of the chair while Kit twisted her hair into four long braids, then wove them together before pinning them in plaited rows across the back of her head.

Rue had never needed braids before; her grandmother always said she sat by Rue's bed at night and combed her long hair so it wouldn't tangle.

"This should stay in place until morning," Kit said.

There was a knock on the door.

Kit cleared her throat and went to answer it. Rue didn't bother turning around when she heard the piece of furniture scraping across the floor as Kit pushed it back into place. Instead, she finished the last bite of her sandwich.

Tension entered the room. She'd have to be dead not to feel it. Rue's spine went straight. She turned just enough to see the two Demons near the door. Dacre had changed his clothes. He was dressed in dark jeans and a jacket. His hair was wet. Rue looked him over, didn't see anything that would allude to all of the noise she'd heard since Dacre had left her here.

"Night is coming," Dacre said, turning dark eyes on Rue. "You must return to the dungeon. Lucifer's orders."

Rue stood and wiped crumbs off her fingers. She turned to Kit. "Thank you." Rue tucked the neatly folded set of pajamas under her arm.

Kit bowed her head slightly. "See you soon."

Rue was tired after the long day, she was grateful to be clean and fed. But she didn't like the sharp smell that wafted into the apartment. It smelled like cleaning supplies.

Dacre and Rue walked in uncomfortable silence. It seemed like the Demon wanted to say something but held it in. Rue had plenty to say but realized it was fruitless. She couldn't beg for her freedom–she'd seen Lucifer, the Demons wouldn't cross him. Rue knew she was shit out of luck unless she could find an escape and run for a portal.

They reached the stairs and began descending. The scent of cleaning supplies burned Rue's nose.

As she stepped off the last stair, Dacre's arm was forcing her toward the door and obstructing her view of the mansion.

"Only look at the door or close your eyes." Dacre was too close. The words brushed against her ear.

Rue turned her head to look down the hall. A hand slapped over her eyes. "I said no."

Rue froze. Before her vision went dark, she'd seen the blood splattered on the walls, floor, and ceiling. Dacre's arm snaked around her middle and lifted Rue off her feet. He carried her out the door like an insolent toddler. "You'll need to learn how to listen." He muttered in her ear before setting her on the stone driveway.

"I'm not a baby," Rue said as she turned to glare at him. "My mother was the Queen of Hell. I've seen things."

Dacre's eyes turned dark. "Do as you're told if you care to live." He brushed past her and opened the door to the lifted Jeep.

Rue climbed up and slid across the seat. "What happened in there?" she asked.

Dacre looked away. "Don't worry about it."

"There was blood everywhere."

Dacre slammed the door and paced behind the Jeep before getting in the driver's seat. Rue watched him warily. Something was off with the Demon. Heat was coming off him in waves. She didn't understand any of it.

Rue buckled her seatbelt, not wanting to receive a head injury from the jostling of the Jeep. She pulled her legs up and crisscrossed them, then held the folded pajamas against her middle like a pillow.

The dead wandered in the road and Dacre was quick to start the Jeep and pull away. Rue turned and watched them follow until they looked like small walking sticks in the distance.

Somehow, Rue drifted off to sleep. She woke to a warm breeze and the soft chirps of crickets. Someone was close, the soft click of the seatbelt releasing woke her fully. She felt an arm stretched across her lap and opened her eyes to the side of Dacre's face. He smelled good, like soap and apple scented shampoo. He went still, realizing she was awake, but that didn't stop Rue from inspecting him closely. There were no scales, no rough skin on his face or hairline.

"It's rude to stare." Dacre pulled away and held the door.

"It's rude to kidnap people," Rue replied.

"Touché." He motioned for her to get out.

"I don't want to go to the dungeon." Rue hugged the pajamas.

"Too bad."

Rue slid out of the seat. She tugged at the jeans that were as size too big for her. She glanced at the forest, didn't notice any of the dead lingering. Hellions caught her eye though. They were watching her. One sniffed the air and took a step forward like a bear ready to pounce.

Rue skipped a step to keep pace with Dacre.

He acted like she didn't exist until he held open the door to the castle and glared down at her.

Rue stopped, glanced over her shoulder at the nearby

forest one last time. The Nightjar's cabin wasn't too far from here. She could run there in less than an hour.

"Don't run," Dacre interrupted her thoughts. "Your mother no longer sits on the throne of Hell which means the dead will go after you." He looked her up and down. "And you don't look like you'd survive five minutes out there alone."

"My mother will kill you," Rue muttered as she walked past Dacre and into the castle. The slippers on her feet making a scuffling sound as she walked.

Dacre muttered something in Hellspeak that sounded like, "Then I can finally rest." Rue wasn't sure if she had the translation correct but the way he sighed made her think it was.

Rue's chest tightened with fear as they moved toward the stairs that spiraled down in to darkness.

As they descended into the dungeon's shadowy depths, Rue's last hope of escaping today slipped away, and the cold, suffocating reality of her capture settled in. She rubbed the runes on her chest. Jed had tried to increase her strength, but she was no match against these monsters. She blinked back tears and wondered if this was how her mother had felt her first time in Hell.

She kept her chin up as she followed Dacre past oily dripping walls and thundering fists pounding on chained doors. Dacre held the dungeon door open, looking away as she walked inside, then he slammed it closed and locked it.

Rue paced her dungeon cell and sat against the wall. She wrapped her arms around herself, rocking against the stone wall until she drifted off to fitful sleep.

———

Everything moved like she was underwater; slow, and fluid. Rue was walking down a cobblestone street, autumn leaves of burnt orange and yellow crunched under her feet. Then she was sitting in a class with an animated professor lecturing on stones in the desert. Then ordering coffee from a cart near the library. She was moving through time in flashes. There was steam in the air and she stepped out of the shower to see a message on a phone but she couldn't make out the text. Anxiety twisted in her stomach. Something smelled like pumpkin coffee. Rue turned and then she was dressed in a costume, her periphery disrupted by the edges of a mask. She searched the cramped room, accepted a cup of beer only to set it down on a nearby table. Young people were surrounding her, dancing. Music boomed from another room. She was having fun, free and smiling behind her mask. She took a small bottle of cinnamon whiskey from her pocket and drank that because it was safe. She danced, felt the beat of the music deep in her chest. Someone touched her shoulder and Rue turned to find a man in a silver mask staring down at her.

Rue woke up with a sharp intake of breath, shivering, despite the warmer pajamas Kit had given her. Rue searched for the cot in the darkness, patting her hand across the stone floor. She touched something soft, recognized it as the jacket she was covered with the other night. She pulled it close and draped it across her body before falling asleep again.

A deep roar woke Rue. She sat up, realizing she was in the cot and not on the floor.

Something shifted in the shadows in the corner of the room. Rue hoped it wasn't a snake or bugs. She shivered before squinting her eyes and focusing.

"You shouldn't sleep on the stone floor," a familiar voice said from the shadows.

"Why should you care?" Rue pulled the blanket around her, rubbed her lips against its softness before remembering it was Dacre's suit jacket. She released the jacket and let it fall to her shoulders.

Dacre stepped out of the shadows. "You sleep with your eyes open."

"No I don't." Rue blinked.

"You do." Dacre was dressed in a suit again. All black.

"No. I don't." Rue snapped. "And why are you watching me sleep like some creepy old man?"

Dacre chuckled darkly. "Get up. It's time to go." He checked his watch. "You've slept too long."

Rue shifted, moving to the edge of the cot, and setting her slippered feet on the damp floor.

From beyond her dungeon cell there was a howling scream. Rue covered her ears and shrank back.

Dacre grabbed her arm and pulled, unwilling to wait for her to get up. "Let's go. The longer you wait the more you'll hear. We need to leave."

Rue tugged her arm back and kicked.

"Stop," Dacre warned, shielding his thigh.

"It doesn't matter, I'm going to die here anyway. Just end it already." Rue punched him in the ribs then kicked his knee with all her might.

Dacre was spitting profanities in Hellspeak and hopping on one foot when a Hellion glanced into the dungeon and laughed.

"Get the fuck out of here," Dacre shouted to the Hellion. He turned to face Rue.

Rue's heart raced; she was breathing in sharp, quick bursts as she backed away from Dacre. The dim light of the dungeon flickered, casting ominous shadows on the stone walls. Dacre stood only a few paces away, his dark eyes fixed on her, unblinking and cold.

"What are you doing?" Dacre asked, his voice smooth, carrying a slight gentle tone, though the threat beneath was clear. The handsome Demon had a gift of threading fine words with threat. He took a step forward, hands raised in a mockery of peace. "Don't even try to fight me. It won't do you any good. You cannot escape this place. You cannot escape *me*."

Something had shifted in Rue during the night. That dream gave her some kind of home for the future which meant she did not stay here. "I'm not going to sit here and wait to be slaughtered by Lucifer. I won't be used by you in the skin trades." Rue shook her head. "That's not happening." Rue's hands trembled but clenched into fists, a fierce determination burned in her center. She had to get out. She had to escape. She had to leave. Now.

Dacre smirked, his head tilting slightly as amusement danced in his dark eyes. "Slaughtered? Is that what you think Lucifer will do to you? That's what he does to the Demons he rules over, makes us suffer. But you, he'll probably end quickly."

Rue didn't reply. Her eyes darted around, searching for

anything she could use as a weapon. But there was nothing. Just him and the walls that felt as though they were closing in.

Dacre lunged.

Rue barely had time to react, diving to the side as his hand reached out to grab her. She stumbled, nearly losing her footing, but she caught herself and whirled around, her pulse pounding in her ears. He was fast.

"I don't want to hurt you," he growled, his earlier calm gone.

Rue's lip curled into a snarl, defiance surging through her. "I'm gonna hurt you."

Without thinking, she charged at him, fists swinging wildly. She knew she was outmatched. Dacre had the strength of a Demon, the speed and the power. But she wasn't going to go down without a fight. She'd fight him every day. Every step of the way.

Her first strike hit his chest, but it felt like hitting stone. A sharp ache spread up her arm. Dacre barely flinched, grabbing her wrist with inhuman speed and twisting it just enough to force a cry of pain from her throat.

"Stop," he ordered, his voice dark and edged with frustration.

Rue twisted in his grip, swinging her other hand up to strike his face. Her knuckles grazed his jaw and to her surprise Dacre stumbled back, releasing her arm. For a brief moment Rue felt the rush of victory, her heart soaring with hope.

But then he came at her again, faster, angrier. "If you are going to act like a child, I will treat you like one." He grabbed her by the shoulders, slamming her back against the stone wall. The impact knocked the air from her lungs and black spots danced in her vision. Dacre's face was inches from hers, his eyes burning with a dangerous mixture of anger and something else she couldn't place.

"You're wasting your energy," he snarled, his breath hot against her skin. "You won't get away."

Rue gasped, struggling in his grip. The stone at her back was cold, pressing into her spine as she fought to free herself, but Dacre was unyielding. His fingers dug into her shoulders, pinning her in place. Desperation flared in her chest as she kicked at him but it only made his hands press her harder against the stone. "You're in a time out." There was a lilt of humor in his tone.

"Let me go!" she screamed, twisting her body.

Dacre didn't move. A dark smile spread across his lips as if he enjoyed the struggle. "I could keep you here forever if I wanted. Do you understand that? You'd never see the light of day. Only darkness. Only the darkest version of the skin trades. I didn't want that for you."

Memories of yesterday flashed through her mind. He had taken her away from the damp dungeon for the day. The threat stung but fueled new anger. Rue's pulse quickened and before she could think it through, she lunged forward, sinking her teeth into the side of his neck with all the strength she had left.

Dacre froze.

For a moment, the taste of blood filled her mouth, metallic and bitter and... sweet. She bit harder, her jaw clenched, and Dacre's hands tightened on her shoulders. A guttural growl emanated from his throat, a sound equal parts pain and rage. His body tensed, his grip went so tight she was afraid he'd break her bones.

He shoved Rue away. Hard. Her head smacked against the stone wall and tiny lights danced in her vision. Rue licked her lips, noticed his blood tasted a lot different than what the Demon at the Black Mansion had forced down her throat. Her legs felt weak, her entire body was trembling. Rue wiped her mouth with the back of her hand, glaring at him, breathing heavily. She glanced down at the smear of blood across the back of her hand and licked it away slowly.

Dacre's hand was pressed to the side of his neck, his eyes wide with shock and fury. Watching her mouth, he moved his hand from his neck and glanced at his palm. Blood dripped. Rue focused on the small bite mark from her teeth. They weren't sharp and the bite was nothing more than blunt marks that had drawn blood.

"You have no fucking idea what you've done," Dacre glowered. "You're going to regret that," he hissed, his voice a low growl.

Dacre stormed out of the dungeon, slamming the door. A heavy lock slid into place.

"Don't let her out," he instructed the Hellion. "Ever."

Rue slid down the wall, her body sore and head aching. She had hurt him, maybe only a little but it was something. Rue touched her lips, watched the blood drip down her fingertips. She licked her lips, then her fingers. She swallowed down every drop of Dacre's blood and wished she had more. What was wrong with her? Her mother and the Hellions drank blood. Plenty of Demons did too. Children didn't. Rue knew why children didn't drink blood. Because it stopped their aging. A million thoughts clouded her mind but she couldn't focus on one of them. She was suddenly very thirsty.

The prisoners in the dungeon started going wild, banging on doors and walls, slamming furniture against the walls, howling and screeching like excited zoo animals.

Twenty-Six

Clea was somewhere dark. She tasted iron, though she hadn't tasted anything since she was alive. This was confusing. Plenty of omens had come to her over the years, visions of a future filled with chaos. She'd shared them but she had never seen herself turned so useless in any omen.

Alastor had done this to her, tried to banish her to the Ether after severing her form with an iron candelabra.

The problem with royal blood was Clea didn't disappear. She was still in the castle, invisible, unable to use her powers. Stuck. But, she'd heard every word from her father, Lucifer. She'd heard him reveal that he killed her, he'd tried to kill Meg and would end this war by killing her grandchildren.

Clea was filled with rage, and she was right to be filled with rage. She roamed the halls of the castle in the burning caves, watching as everything changed; the walls shifted, the grounds bubbled with magma, the Hellions and Demons transfigured into sinister forms. It was worse than before, much worse. Clea had spent enough time with her father to know that Lucifer was ready for war; she saw his tricks, too bad she could do nothing to help. She could only watch.

Now she was trapped between realms. Present in Hell but unable to speak with anyone or move anything. She'd watched hopelessly as Rue had attempted to escape the man in the suit. Something was off about that Demon, Clea could tell just by looking at him. She wasn't even sure he was a true Demon.

———

Then

Rue sat cross-legged on the bed, a blanket draped around her shoulders like a cloak, eyes wide with lingering traces of sleep. Across from her Clea sat in the same position, so pale that she might drift away into nothingness. Clea was a ghost. Rue didn't know any different-her grandmother had always been a ghost, it was the normal way of things in her world.

"Grandma, it felt so real," Rue whispered, leaning closer. Her small voice filled the quiet room, her words soft but urgent. "I saw you there, in my dream. You were... you were fighting. There were so many shadows, but you–" she paused, struggling to find the right words, "you were shining and then you disappeared. Forever." Tears glistened in Rue's eyes. "I don't want you to disappear forever."

"Oh, child," Clea's red lips curled into a slight smile, her gaze softened. "Dreams are strange things, my sweet

Rue," she murmured, waving a graceful hand as if to brush Rue's recollection away like dust. "They're clouds; shifting, drifting, always changing shape. Just wisps of thoughts."

But Rue's brow furrowed in frustration. "No, this was different," she insisted, her small fists balling in her lap. "You were helping mother. You used your magic, and there was this... this light around you. And you were fighting–" her voice dropped to a whisper, "–you were fighting a giant bad man. I think it was Lucifer."

Clea's ghostly form stilled, though her gentle smile remained. "A giant, angry man?" she said, her tone casual, though Rue noticed the slightest flicker in her grandmother's eyes. "Oh, child. In the realm of Hell, there are plenty big, strong men and Demons who frighten the strong and tempt the brave. But that is a distant worry, far from us now. We have the Hellions who will do everything to protect you. And your mother. She is the strongest woman I've ever met. And she killed Lucifer a long time ago. He can't hurt any of us now."

Rue nodded, though a hint of disappointment glimmered in her wide eyes. "It's just... I felt like you were really there, like I was seeing something real. I could smell smoke and blood. There were so many people. Angels and Demons. Mother was there, fighting with... I don't know what he was."

"Tell me," Clea urged.

Rue blinked a few times, collecting her thoughts. "He was like an Angel but black wings. He saved her."

"Saved who, dear?"

"Mother." Rue swallowed and toyed with the edge of her blanket.

"You have more to say?" Clea asked.

Rue nodded, dark hair falling over her left eye. "I'm afraid."

Clea leaned closer, her gaze warm and unwavering. "Rue," she said softly, her voice lilting like a distant melody, "even if your dream were true, even if I could help in such a way—my time for such things has long passed."

Rue frowned, her small face set with stubbornness that made Clea chuckle softly. "But you're still here," she argued, tugging her blanket tighter as if seeking reassurance. "You're still here with me."

Clea reached out, touching Rue's cheek. "For now, yes," she agreed, her voice softer than before. "But remember, my love, dreams have a way of playing with what we wish for. They show us glimmers, but we must live in the world we have."

Rue fell quiet, her little shoulders dropping under the weight of her grandmother's words. Clea gave a final, comforting smile before reaching forward and moving the child to her lap. "Don't trouble yourself over it, darling," she said gently. "Time will reveal what it wishes, and you will be ready, just as you need to be."

Clea smoothed her cold hands over Rue's dark hair. "Now, tell me more about the Angel with black wings. He can't hurt you. Skeele will keep you safe. And so will Chel. You know Chel thinks you are the sweetest little thing he's ever seen before, like a kitten. No one will let harm come to you." Clea adjusted the blanket to cover Rue's bare neck so she wouldn't catch a chill. "What did he look like?"

Rue raised one arm silently and pointed at the little boy sleeping in the bed across the room.

"Remm?" Clea asked. "The Angel with black wings looked like your brother?"

Rue nodded silently.

"Okay," Clea exhaled. "But you said he saved your mother?"

Rue nodded again.

"Good." Clea wrapped her arms around Rue and hugged her.

"You helped save them too," Rue whispered. "I saw you."

Twenty-Seven

A sound like paper tearing echoed across the Earthen plane. Grandmother Crow looked out the window and up at the sky, not assuming the noise was thunder. That was anything but thunder. The sound came with the shuffling of heavy feet, hooved, padded, booted from creatures the Earthen plane had never seen before.

Grandmother Crow knew demonic forces gathering. She'd seen the stories in the papers of storms and illness the past few days. Diseases that had been long forgotten had suddenly returned. Floods in the mountains and heat like never before struck the coastline. Strange creatures caused destruction in small towns. Something dark was taking over and spilling onto the Earthen plane.

Hosa's eyes narrowed at the sky. "Ah what has the Allegewi done?"

"No, not him," Grandmother Crow reached for a shotgun and locked the kitchen door. She shivered, noticing a shadow that looked like a hyena ran across the yard. "This is something darker. I fear this Earth is melding with something treacherous."

Elsu and Jacy set down their cards and focused on the sound of the wind whistling through the pines. There was plenty more movement they could discern besides the pine needle-hush.

Grandmother Crow turned to her sons and cocked the shotgun. "This will be difficult without Iye. We will be fully outnumbered very soon."

She glanced at the picture of her long dead son, killed by Demons while rescuing Nicholas and Janet's daughter who'd been kidnapped years ago. None of them had seen Shay since, but every so often she'd send a postcard or call.

Elsu stood, downed the last of the whiskey in his glass and slammed it on the table. "We've been waiting for retribution for a long time." Elsu glanced at his brother's picture and the empty seat at the table that had collected dust over the years.

"I told you the Allegewi would bring war," Hosa said with an anger filled voice.

Grandmother Crow was quick to slam her fist on the counter. "This is not the war of one Allegewi. Jed did not bring this. You forgave him once. He might be the only one who can save us." She pointed out the window. "Or maybe Shay."

Hosa bit back words he wanted to spit in vengeance. He knew Jed wasn't the cause, but he wanted to blame his brother's death on someone.

Wind slammed against the door, threatening to blast it open. Nails scraped against glass. A cluster of moving shadows scrambled toward the single light in the backyard.

A crashing sound echoed like a shutter stuck in the wind. The light in the backyard went out with the shattering of glass.

"Now, boys," Grandmother Crow warned as she picked up satchels of powder, tucking them in her apron. "We need to leave this place." She felt the darkness encroaching, knew the sound of claws scraping against the windows of their secluded house in the Montana reservation.

"The others–" Jacy started to say.

"They're dead." Grandmother Crow's voice was dire. "There is no one but us." She filled her apron pockets with shotgun shells. "This is worse than when the dead walked. The devil has sent creatures not of this realm."

Elsu, Hosa, and Jacy canvassed the old house, collecting every stashed gun and knife.

They met at the door that opened to the driveway.

Grandmother Crow was chanting, her hand filled with dark powder. She nodded to Hosa, who opened the door. Hot air blasted into the house, and with it came a high pitched squeal of excited creatures ready for their next meal.

Hosa turned to Jacy. "You make sure she gets to the truck."

Jacy nodded and moved closer to his mother.

Something from the shadows was running full bore toward the door. They all saw it, a creature like a hyena with blackened skin and sharp teeth. It yapped as it leapt toward the door opening. Grandmother Crow threw the handful of black powder at the creature. It dropped to the ground with a whine that could be heard for miles. Elsu shot the creature, blasting it's head off the neck.

"Now," Grandmother Crow said, running out the door behind Hosa.

They made it to the truck, the shadows keeping their distance after seeing what happened to the creature at the door.

Hosa got behind the wheel and started the engine. Jacy opened the door and helped Grandmother Crow into the backseat.

Elsu was last after letting off a few blasts from his shotgun. He opened the passenger side door, black ichor dripping down his arms. "Go. Go. Go!" Elsu shouted. His face was pale as though he'd seen something not meant for human eyes.

Hosa kicked the truck into gear and sped away.

"Where do we go?" Hosa asked as they cleared the reservation and made it to the highway, swerving around broken down vehicles.

Grandmother Crow was wringing her hands. She had a bad feeling. The worst feeling. Their home was being destroyed quickly. Creatures of all sizes ran in the shadows like packs of venomous dogs. Every so often, they saw one of the walking dead ambling on the side of the road.

"Mother?" Hosa urged after she hadn't replied to him for minutes.

Grandmother Crow cleared her throat. "Get to a crossroads. We must call upon Nero and Shay." A hard shiver ran up her spine and across her shoulders. "I fear that we may meet Iye very soon."

Twenty-Eight

The Basilisk stirred, curling its immense, scaled body along the parched riverbed, where dry cracks spiderwebbed across the mud. The Black River, once coursing thick and dark through the Adirondacks of Hell, lay silent. The Basilisk slithered between pine trees, watching. Its glossy black scales reflected the faint, ever-bleeding red of Hellsky as it raised its massive head, forked tongue flickering to taste the stale, smoky air.

Then, a scent—a faint, familiar trace woven through the air—made the Basilisk's nostrils flare and its pale eyes narrow with recognition. Meg. She had returned.

Slowly, the Basilisk began to move, each ripple of its muscular length carving a path through the brittle forest floor, splintering dried branches and scattering leaves like ash in its wake. The trees twisted away, bowing to the creature's passage. The Basilisk emitted an odd, almost eager energy, gliding in winding curves that quickened as it scented Meg closer with each mile through the dark woods.

It slithered through forests and open roads, through

fields turned to ash and around pools of magma. The sharp silence of Hell in waiting was broken only by the soft, rhythmic scrape of scales over stone. The Basilisk was headed somewhere with a purpose–its singular purpose since Meg's presence had returned to Hell's tortured land. Lucifer might have reclaimed the throne, but it was Meg the creature sought, a beacon that called it like a master's whistle.

TWENTY-NINE

MEG

THE BABYLON FOUNTAIN stands before us, glistening ominously under the dim light, its waters an eerie mirror to the dark realm we are about to enter.

I glance over my shoulder at the others–Chel, Nightingale, Noah, Jed, Shay, Thrush, and Remington–all resolute, faces set with grim determination. My eyes fall on Sparrow, clad in shadowed armor, his eyes sharp and ready. The Legion of Angels are behind him. All this time we fought against his family curse and never focused on the reality: my bloodline is cursed just as deep. My mother, dead. My first child, dead. My daughter, kidnapped. I can feel in my bones that death will come for me before this battle is over. It has come for me many times. On that stairwell in Gouverneur. In that little hospital when John Lewis held a pillow over my face. The moment when the Raven King stabbed me to death. I glance at my son; all these years I kept him hidden away, protected, his true identity concealed... I should have done the same for her. I grip the Basilisk blade at my side. She will not find the same fate as the rest of us.

"No one separates unless necessary. Rue's priority. We get her and get out," Sparrow says firmly, tracing the plan in the air as he speaks. He turns to his Legion Commander who bows his head in silent understanding, stepping back to prepare.

I take a deep breath, my heart beating loudly against my ribs. My gaze shifts to Remington. Reaching out, I pull him close, holding his face in my hands, memorizing each line. "Be careful," I whisper, my voice only loud enough for him to hear. "Stay close to me. Promise?"

Remington offers me a half-smile, filled with familiar bravado, his eyes serious. "I will. I promise. A promise is a promise."

My breath catches before I repeat the phrase. "A promise is a promise." I glance at Sparrow and nod.

With a unified, collective, steeling breath, we plunge into the fountain.

———

THE PLUNGE into Hell is instantaneous. The fading light blinks out as the heavy atmosphere swallows us. But... something is wrong. I am not met with the cool water of the Nightjar's pond, instead something dark and thick coats my body. Remington's hand slips out of mine as we try to swim through the thickness. There's dirt in my mouth, grit in my eyes. This is not the murky water of the Nightjar's pond. It's mud. Clinging to us, dragging us down. My lungs burn as I try and swim through it, grabbing handfuls and pulling myself up. I finally break the surface, wipe the mud off my face, and gasp. Thicker than pudding it clings to me, my feet sunk deep–but I can feel the bottom. I'm near the shore at least. I stagger, gasping, the mud pulling at my ankles, it's cold grip relentless. Around me, the others break the surface, gasping and moaning. They are trapped, the mud spread out like a vast mire, swallowing everyone.

I struggle to the shore, stretch out flat and grab a tree root, then pull myself in. The mud threatens to keep my boots as I pull my feet free with a sucking sound. My eyes dart around and I catch the panic in Remington's face as he fights to free himself. Thrush is nearby, calm as he scans the shore and moves to his back to float.

"Remm," Thrush calls. "Don't struggle, it will pull you under."

Remington freezes still and glances to Thrush, then tries to maneuver his body to float on his back.

Sparrow is a short distance away, his movements growing sluggish as the mud pulls him deeper.

With one final heave, I manage to wrench myself free and scramble forward onto firmer ground. I look back, heart hammering. This is a shit show. An absolute shit show if I ever saw one. The Basilisk tooth blade is gone, sunk in the mud.

I glance to Remington, then Sparrow, swallowing. Dread is slicing through me.

Sparrow holds my gaze, his expression with steady assurance. "Get the boys first," he rasps. "I'm not going anywhere." He stops struggling in the thick mud, sinking to his jawline.

I search the area, looking for a way to get them out. There's a fallen sapling, half burned. I grab it, maneuver toward Remington and drop it, holding the shoreline end.

"Pull yourself in," I say. "Hurry."

Remington rolls to his stomach and I am filled with relief as he grips the end of the sapling and begins pulling himself to shore.

I stand on the end, holding it down, and take in the scene. Sparrow is slowly drowning. There is no sign of Noah or Nightingale, but since they are ghosts they might have traveled to another realm to escape the mud. Chel is wading in the middle, giving orders to the Raven King's Legion. There's too much panic. Some are already dead, their faces blue and frozen in time. Shay comes through, her blue hair coated with mud. Panicked eyes take in the mess we've stepped into.

"Float on your back, Shay," Chel says as he reaches for her. "Don't struggle against it. Where's the half-breed?"

"He was right behind me," Shay's voice is strained as she struggles against the mud.

A head breaks the surface not far from Chel. Chel reaches out and grabs the back of the man's jacket, lifting him above the surface.

It's Jed. I glance at Shay who is taking a sigh of relief.

Remington makes it to shore.

The mud is up to Sparrow's ears. He points to Thrush, eyes dark.

I move the sapling closer to Thrush and he grabs the end. Remington helps me hold the opposite end as Thrush drags himself in. My arms burn with strain.

"Hurry up," Remington urges. "My dad is dying.

Again." He chuckles as Thrush swears and drags himself faster.

"You're a real sick fuck," Thrush snaps.

Remington shrugs. "Learned it from you."

Thrush makes it to shore and catches his breath as Remington moves the sapling closer to Sparrow. I am glad to see the bow and arrows didn't get lost.

The mud is over Sparrow's ears. Over his mouth. He only has one hand above the surface. The sapling lands just out of reach of his fingertips.

Panic rises in my chest as his fingertips reach and miss and reach again. Pained eyes glance at me. I don't think he ever considered death by mud. But who would? It's a shit way to die.

We move the sapling closer, Remington and Thrush stepping into the mud, their feet sinking.

A set of green eyes are watching me. The mud is slowly consuming him as he sinks further, the surface coating his cheekbones, nearing the crescent of his lower eyelid.

"Grab it!" Remington shouts.

"Reach for it, Sparrow!" I shout. "Grab the end."

Slowly, achingly slow, his hand moves and he grips the end of the sapling just before closing his eyes and going under.

"Pull!" Remington shouts.

The three of us pull him in. Sparrow's grip remains strong as we drag him through the mud. As he gets closer to the shore, he is nothing but a giant mass of mud-covered Angel slowly being dragged in.

Thirty

At last, through the thinning line of dead trees, the Basilisk spotted her, a familiar figure standing against the burnt landscape. There were flickers of firelight from the distant, smoky horizon. She was covered in mud. The Basilisk slowed, lowering its enormous head to meet her gaze, a strange glint of devotion shimmering in its pale, unblinking eyes.

With a gentleness belying its monstrous form, it curled around her feet, body looping in heavy, rippling coils, waiting for her acknowledgment. Its large head rested mere inches from Meg's hand with its long fangs sheathed and jaw relaxed in a rare display of trust and submission, an unspoken loyalty in the creature's silent, expectant stare.

Meg's hand hesitated only a moment before resting lightly on the Basilisk's head, feeling the cool, ridged scales beneath her palm. She gave the Basilisk a small, steady nod, and it responded with a soft rumble, almost a purr, vibrating through the ground beneath them.

"You came," she murmured. "Can you help the

others?" She pointed to the Legion warriors sinking in the mud of the Nightjar's pond, so thick it was, like a bog or quicksand; bottomless, wanting to consume.

The Basilisk unfurled from around her feet and floated toward the warriors that were still alive. Chel grabbed on with a hearty groan, one arm circled around the Basilisk's middle, the other he used to grab hands and tug up. Then the Basilisk pulled them free and deposited them on the burnt land near the pond. The creature made three passes over the mud, pausing for those stuck to grab onto it or for Chel to help. He even dragged in a few of the dead ones.

"No. No. He's dead!" Shay screamed.

Chel grumbled something in Hellspeak before dropping to his knees next to Jed. "A little mud can't have killed you, weak fuck."

Shay was crying, wiping mud from Jed's face.

Chel slammed his fist down on Jed's chest in some form of archaic and violent resuscitative effort.

It worked.

Jed gasped, sitting up with wide eyes and rubbing his chest. "What the hell was that for?"

"To bring you away from the light, clotpole." Chel stood, the giant Hellion taking a look at the Angels cleaning their wings and making it to their feet. Half were missing their weapons. "Goddamn," Chel muttered. He ran a hand down his leg, relieved to feel his weapon in the holster.

THIRTY-ONE

MEG

As SPARROW's body is dragged in completely, I dash closer to him, grabbing onto his arms with desperate urgency. I wipe the mud from his mouth and nose and eyes.

"Please be alive," I mutter. "You can't die now you big stupid bird." I shake his shoulders.

Bright green eyes flash open. "It's our wings," he says softly, dirt caking his lips and sticking to his teeth. "Lucifer knew we'd die in the mud. Never stood a chance." Sparrow struggles to sit up, reaches over his shoulder, and spreads one of his wings out to drip the mud off. "It coats the feathers." He points at Chel. "The Hellion doesn't have feathers so he made it to the surface." He nods to me and the boys. "You all don't have wings. I'd say, no more travel by water."

"Yeah, sure, whatever," I agree. "Because I'm not traveling fucking anywhere until I get my daughter back."

Sparrow stands and shakes his wings. "Let's move. Rue doesn't have time for us to slow down."

I catch his gaze, my chest tightening at the near miss. A quick nod from the others communicates that they are shaken but intact. The bodies of the dead Angels will have to stay.

We take a few steps, scanning the landscape, shadows thickening around us as we start for the burning heart of Hell.

Heavy footsteps from the nearby forest draw our attention. A sickening feeling fills my stomach as we brace ourselves for what is about to come through.

———

"Nero!" Shay announces.

The giant horse gallops closer. There's a man on his back, missing a leg, a pointed prosthetic in its place. His face looks vague, like everyone and anyone. I can't place him.

Sparrow reaches for me. "How are you here?" Sparrow asks the man.

He's looking down at us, face pale and pained. He struggles to get off Nero's back and lands with an indignant thump.

"I knew the horse would bring me to you," pegleg says.

"There is no way you are real." Sparrow is glaring now.

The man smiles slightly before wagging a finger in our direction. "That's true. I shouldn't be alive. But there are forces at work here. Something bigger than just us and I was saved."

"Who is he?" I ask.

"A Deacon," Sparrow replies.

"Not just any Deacon," the man says. "The *last* Deacon." He claps his hands together. "Now." He looks around us at the Legion. "I was hoping for more troops but it shouldn't be a problem." He groans, walking closer. "Let's go to war." His common face splits into a dark smile.

"Nero," Shay is out of breath after helping Jed to his feet. "Destroy the portal." She points at the muddy pond.

Nero shakes his head, his entire body shivering and shuddering as he changes forms.

None of us want to risk death by mud if anyone comes through that pond again.

Nero gallops toward the pond then blows fire over it until it is nothing more than baked dirt, hardened and cracking.

"Could've used that trick while heating up your pizzas," Noah's voice breaks the silence.

I turn to find Nightingale fussing over Thrush and Noah taking in the scene and the dead Angels.

"Good, you're back," I say.

"Good. You're alive." Noah brushes a hand through his hair. "We got really worried about that mud. Couldn't make it through." He looks me over. "Seems you made it out okay."

Breath escapes my chest as a half laugh. "Yeah, I made it out just fine."

Noah nods, cautious eyes search my face. "Let's go get your girl."

Thirty-Two

Hell stretched out before them, a landscape twisted by Lucifer's return. The sky burned crimson, split by blackened lightning, and the ground was a shattered wasteland littered with cracked and oozing molten rivers.

Meg moved swiftly with Remington at her side and Sparrow on her left.

The Basilisk slithered alongside them, its scaled body whispering over rock and ruin, eyes glowing with a predatory light.

Ahead, the familiar path was littered with the dead stumbling through the debris, drawn to the pulse of life that dared to invade their corrupted domain.

The Deacon was riding Nero and raised a hand, veering them away. The dead had collected to the greatest numbers ever. Hell had all the power without the Deacons to sort souls and send them to their rightful place.

Several of the undead sensed their presence, emitting hollow, gurgling cries as they lunged forward.

"We can't avoid them all," Sparrow muttered, drawing

his weapon. The Legion behind him followed suit, their weapons raised, sending the walking dead to a future of eternal darkness.

Magic crackled in Jed's fingertips. Shay touched his side and whispered, "Save your energy."

Meg waved everyone forward, eager to find her daughter and end this war. They left crumbles of mud as it dried and flaked off them like evening snow.

The group pushed forward, exhausted but determination burning brighter than ever.

Sparrow and Chel watched the sky for Hellions and Demons, but it was eerily silent.

"He's expecting us." Sparrow's voice is deep with worry. He gripped his weapon, the Basilisk tooth blade strapped to his thigh, ready for use.

They waited at the sparse treeline, the castle in the burning caves ahead. It loomed above them, a fortress of stone and flame. A broken home. The air was thick with heat, shadows dancing along the cave walls whispering chants of the devil who now ruled.

Meg stepped forward into the clearing, heart thundering in her chest. She may not have wings, she may have lost her power to travel and *poof*, but she had none of that when she killed seven Hellions who came to slaughter her on the Earthen plane. She had none of that and she survived true evil and darkness.

This. Was. Nothing.

———

"LUCIFER!" Meg shouted. "Grandfather! Come out and face us! Come out of that cave and bring me my daughter!"

There was a beat of silence, the kind that stretched too far and too long. A hush of wings echoed across the royal grounds. A dark shadow circled overhead.

Sparrow took the Basilisk blade out of its holster and passed it to Meg.

Everyone readied themselves with the Raven King's forged blades. Or at least, those who hadn't lost them to the pond.

A dark chuckle echoed before the shadow landed on the balcony of the ballroom, crumbling walls as his backdrop. Lucifer's form was radiant with an unholy light. His dark hair framed a face that was both beautiful and monstrous, his eyes holding a fire that promised destruction.

"Granddaughter!" Lucifer shouted across the grounds as he leaned casually against the balcony baluster. "You always did have a flare for dramatics. Your mother too. But, what makes you think you've earned an audience?" His smile was sharp. "Rue is... indisposed at the moment."

Meg's grip tightened on the Basilisk blade, rage boiled in her veins. "Give her to me!"

Lucifer straightened, clapping his hands mockingly. "Oh, you want a fight." He leaned to the side, eyes narrowing at the forms in the treeline. "What have you brought me? More souls? Is this a trade? I've plenty without the Deacons but my strength can only grow. I'll gladly take whoever you are hiding behind you." He laughed.

Meg held her ground, never taking her eyes off Lucifer,

but she heard the footfalls as those she brought began stepping out of the treeline and revealing themselves.

"Oh!" Lucifer clapped his hands like a kid at Christmas. "You brought me a *Raven King*. Oooh, he's worth *millions of souls*. A perfect sacrifice." He swung his legs over the baluster and balanced on the edge of the balcony. "What else have you got there? Children? What the fuck is wrong with you, Meg? Bringing children to a war."

Remington and Thrush stepped forward, weapons gripped in strong hands. They were far from young boys–they were nearly men now and they'd come for vengeance. They'd come to reclaim their home. They'd come to protect those they loved.

Lucifer held his hand over his eyes as though to shade out the ocher sunlight of Hell. "What is that?" he pointed at Remington. "Is that... oh, it can't be. I never even heard a whisper about *that one*. I would have taken that one too. Hm. Too bad really. He would have looked nice in my dungeon. He's still young enough to mold into something else. He's still young enough to turn to *destruction*. I never thought you'd do that, Meg. Never thought you'd bring a Shadow Heir straight to my door. This is the best sacrifice I've ever received." He laughed excitedly.

"You will not have him. You will not take any of them!" Meg bent her knees, ready for whatever came next. "Now shut your filthy fucking mouth and give me back my daughter!"

Lucifer straightened, clapping his hands mockingly. "Oh, you really do want a fight? Well, you shall get one."

He gestured, and from the shadows emerged an army of Hellions and Demons. Creatures forged from infernal magic with twisted form and eyes aflame with malice poured out in a flood of darkness, weapons raised, and the battlefield quaking beneath their advance.

Sparrow stepped beside Meg, ready.

Meg's throat felt thick as she envisioned all of her children dying today. She glanced to Sparrow, and he shook his head.

"You've battled worse. This is nothing." He smirked, winked, showed sharp teeth. "These are weapons as well."

Meg nodded in understanding.

A row of Hellions charged, roaring and growling like wild things. Footsteps came from behind Meg and Sparrow as the Raven King's Legion moved ahead to fight.

Smaller, lesser Demons scrambled toward Meg, Sparrow, and the others. Their clawed feet scraping against the ashen ground. The horde moved like a swarm, their twisted forms distorted by the pulsing Hellfire that sprouted up around them. Their eyes glinted with a frenzied hunger, their jagged teeth gnashed as they closed in, eager to rend and tear.

The Angels fought expertly, their movements a blur of grace and lethal precision. Wings unfurled in flashes of white and gold and mud as they cleaved through Hellion flesh. Similarly, Hellion weapons cleaved through Angel flesh, each strike sending a ripple of light through the air, momentarily illuminating the battlefield.

Sparrow's sword sliced through the small Demons that lunged for his legs, their bodies disintegrating into ash as they hit the ground. He kept moving, each step careful but forceful, as he shielded Meg's side. His blade glowed as it cut through another Demon, the ichor sizzling off its enchanted edge.

"Keep close!" He shouted, his voice strained with effort.

Meg nodded, her weapon arcing through the air as she brought down a Demon that had managed to slip past Sparrow. Her breath came in short gasps, but she forced herself to stay steady, to remain a pillar of strength for the others. She gritted her teeth and pushed forward even as more Demons poured from the shadows.

Thrush and Remington fought alongside them, a deadly pair with skills honed by countless days of training. Thrush's blade struck a demon with flawless precision. Demons crumpled and dissolved, but for every one they struck down, two more seemed to take its place.

Jed's hands were aglow with battle magic as he sent bolts of fire and electricity to the surrounding Demons and Hellions, holding back the line.

Thrush and Remington stood back-to-back, covering each other's blind spots. A Demon with wings of leathery sinew swooped toward them, but Thrush sheathed his blade then ducked low, readying his bow and sent an arrow straight into its eye. It let out a shriek before crashing to the ground.

"Is it me or are these things multiplying?" Remington grunted.

Thrush shot him a grim look. "It's not just you."

Nightingale and Noah fought around the boys, taking down bodies with blades and astral magic of firebolts and fire.

Meg moved forward, but a Demon sprang up from the ground, claws reaching for her face. Before she could react,

Sparrow was there, cutting it down with a swift, brutal strike. He glanced over his shoulder, sweat and ash streaking his face.

"You good?" he asked, voice tight with worry.

Meg swallowed and steadied herself. "Still standing." Her blade swept out to catch another Demon.

Meanwhile, Chel fought like a whirlwind, his weapon spinning deadly arcs. He parried a blow from a Demon wielding a jagged spear, then countered with a strike that sent the creature sprawling. Nearby, Shay reloaded her pistol, and took note of how many bullets she had left. She glanced to the Deacon hanging back with Nero. The urge to change forms tingled the back of her neck. The Demon poison in the scar on her thigh burned with fury. She wasn't sure how long she could hold off.

Jed's battle magic left the ground scorched and smoking.

Despite their fierce resistance, the lesser Demons kept coming, their screeching cries echoing in the fiery darkness. The group pressed on, knowing that every second counted to Rue. They must reach the castle.

But the deeper they fought into Hell's twisted battle-field, the more desperate the Hellions and Demons became, as if driven by a force greater than themselves. Too many replenished. Too many Angels were dying. It was easy to see, they were quickly losing this battle and yet they were so far from the castle in the burning caves.

The last row of Angel Legion faced off with endless rows of Hellions and Demons.

Meg glanced to Remington. A sickening feeling gnawed

at her gut. "You run away. You live in hiding if we fall," she mouthed to her son.

Remington coldly shook his head no.

Lucifer laughed over the battlefield before taking flight. He circled above the fighting.

Angels dropped and soon there were no more than a few dozen standing between Meg and hundreds of Hellions.

Just as the Hellions charged, a beam of light split the forest behind them, and the losing edge of the battlefield was bathed in brilliance. Gabriel stepped forward, wings outstretched and armor gleaming, his expression a mixture of fierce resolve and holy wrath. Behind him, a Legion of Angels advanced. Their ranks stretched as far as the eye could see.

Gabriel's voice boomed across the battlefield. "That is no way to speak to a lady!"

Lucifer smiled darkly, lifting an arm and calling upon hundreds more Hellions and Demons.

"She is far from a lady." Lucifer landed on the battlefield. "A lady wouldn't kill her grandfather. A lady wouldn't take all she'd been given and destroy it. A lady would not give these creatures hope that they deserved something better. A lady of darkness would not turn Hell into some... refuge."

Gabriel shrugged nonchalantly before turning to Sparrow. "We are late because the Nightjar's pond is gone. Completely disappeared."

Sparrow motioned to the dried mud on his clothing. "There was an incident."

Gabriel motioned for the army to move forward. "We had to use a portal halfway across Hell."

He took in Meg's form, coated in battle fluids, sweating, rasping breath. He nodded. "The Seven Kingdoms of Heaven have sent warriors."

"All seven?" Meg asked, unbelieving.

"All seven," Gabriel said. He glanced to Thrush, then the young man who looked very much like the Raven King. He paused a moment too long before joining the army of Angels.

It wasn't long before the battlefield was coated in a thick sludge of blood and ichor from Angels and Demons alike as they perished in battle. Everyone surviving was covered in a film of sweat and gore. Meg was closer to the castle than ever before, Hellions charged her only to be struck down by her Basilisk, who'd joined in the fight.

———

THE LAST DEACON gripped Nero's black mane, heart thundering against his ribs, stump aching as it rubbed against the wooden prosthetic. The battlefield before them was a seething chaos of fire and shadows, the sky above streaked with crimson as if Hell itself was bleeding. The Deacon's ancient magic pulsed through his veins, the weight of centuries pressing on his soul, but he drew strength from it. This was his purpose, his final stand against the darkness that threatened to consume them all. He had to maintain the balance.

He leaned forward and whispered in Nero's ear. "I think now is the time."

Nero snorted, his nostrils flaring, sensing the tension and power in the air. The Demon horse's hooves thundered against the scorched earth as he charged forward, slicing through the thick clouds of ash and smoke.

Nero didn't like watching Shay risk her life like she was. He wanted to be by her side but the white horse had given him duty. He had the key and the guide; the secret to defeating Lucifer.

"Giddy up," the Deacon patted Nero and twisted his hands in Nero's mane, holding on as Nero ran into the battlefield.

The Deacon's cloak billowed behind him as he whispered an incantation older than time itself. The air around them hummed, vibrating with the potency of his magic.

Nero jumped over fighting warriors, weaved around charging Hellions, moved so fast the only one who kept a close eye on him was the fallen Archangel who'd been consumed by darkness.

Ahead, Lucifer stood at the heart of the battlefield, his presence an unholy beacon. His form radiated malevolence, a towering figure of black wings and burning eyes. He watched their approach with an expression of twisted amusement, as though the Deacon's defiance was nothing more than fleeting entertainment.

The Deacon lifted one hand, symbols of ancient power glowing around his fingers. He was prepared to unleash power that could unmake the fabric of reality itself, power born from the dawn of creation. His lips parted, ready to release that incantation that would strike at Lucifer's very core and end this war and seal the shredded Veil between realms.

But Lucifer moved with a speed that defied belief.

In the space between one heartbeat and the next, he crossed the distance. Nero reared, trying to throw himself backward, but Lucifer's hand was already there, gripping the Deacon's throat. The Deacon continued his chant, voice scraped, air barely moving through his windpipe. Lucifer took the Deacon to the air for all to see and the battlefield went still.

The Deacon's eyes widened in shock, and the power he had summoned dissipated, leaving him defenseless before he ever had the chance to use it.

"No," was the Deacon's last gasp.

Lucifer's lips curled into a mockery of a smile. "Did you really think you could stop me?" His voice was velvet; cruel and dark and full of mirth. With the flick of his wrist, he drove his other hand forward, a blade of pure hellfire piercing through the Deacon's chest.

The Deacon's vision blurred. Pain seared through him as his life force slipped away like sand through fingers. He tried to speak, tried to call on the magic of the Deacons one last time, but it was too late. The light in his eyes dimmed and his body went slack. Lucifer held the Deacon's body out for all to see, shook him like a fish on a pole. Then Lucifer released him and the Deacon fell lifelessly to the charred battlefield.

Nero's eyes went wide with disbelief. The white horse had told him. The key and the guide would save them...

The Deacon was the answer. But now he was dead. Nero trotted backward, gathered fire in his throat, and made his way to Shay. There was no way out of this war now. No way out besides death and he was not going to let Shay die amongst Demons and Angels.

THIRTY-THREE

MEG

I watch, horrified as the last Deacon falls from Hellsky. Shit. There goes our secret weapon. There's still too many Hellions between me and Lucifer. Definitely more than seven. Too many bodies between me and the castle.

It all feels so defeating, watching that blasted Deacon fall from the sky like a sack of shit.

"We didn't need him," Sparrow says. "We will be invincible together." He wipes gore from his cheek but I catch his absent gaze as he internally recalculates how close to defeat we actually are.

"I don't think this is the time for omens delivered by feather." I wipe my hands on my dirty pants and try to quell the growing unease in my center.

I glance over my shoulder and take inventory. Shay is moving toward me, a smile on her face.

Nero gallops close to her.

"Don't worry, Meg," Shay smiles before brushing blue hair out of her face. There is a strange twinkling in her eyes. "You don't need a Deacon, you've got a Demon-stained girl and her trusty Crossroads Demon-horse."

"I don't understand." I search her face for a clue but I get nothing.

Sparrow slashes at a tiny Demon biting the toe of my boot. I kick the carcass away.

Shay nods to Nero before her body flickers and wavers. She changes before my eyes. Suddenly she's tall, hair so blue and wild, eyes darker than night. She isn't a terrifying Demon like Nero, no, she is a warrior; intimidating and absolutely stunning.

"Oh my god," I whisper. "You're amazing."

Shay smiles before chanting, "Out of the eater will come something to eat. And out of the strong will come something sweet."

The ground smokes. Brimstone fills the air. The ground vibrates under our feet.

"Out of the eater will come something to eat. And out of the strong will come something sweet. Out of the eater will come something to eat. And out of the strong will come something sweet. Out of the eater will come something to eat. And out of the strong will come something sweet." Shay chants it over and over again, her eyes glinting.

Nero whinnies something dark and guttural before pointing his muzzle to Hellsky and releasing a steady stream of fire.

My pupils blow wide as I take in the scene before me.

Figures begin appearing behind her. Hundreds—no, thousands. Some, I recognize. Some I've never seen before.

"I have my own army," Shay says proudly. "Thousands of souls from Crossroads deals."

Nero snorts.

"And a dragon horse," Shay says, patting his flank.

"Okay." I nod, barely believing.

"Oh, one more thing." Shay holds out her hand. "Out of the eater will come something to eat. And out of the strong will come something *sweet*."

The Deacon appears next to her; the one whom we just watched fall from the sky like a sack of shit. He looks at me, then in the direction of Lucifer.

Nero whinnies and stomps his hooves with joy.

The bodies don't stop appearing. Men and women. Demons. Angels. And... Hellions. Oh my god, Hellions! My Hellions.

A lump forms in my throat. I swallow it down because girls like me don't cry. We don't cry when the Hellions who gave their lives to save me come back from the dead.

Klaus smiles and waves. Tukka salutes me. And then...

"No," I whisper, walking closer.

He moves forward, men and women and Demons parting to let *him* through. I hold my breath, recognizing the curled horns, the broad shoulders, the sharp-toothed smile.

"Skeele!"

Skeele walks toward me, arms out. Last time I saw him he was dying. Skinned. Bloodied. He was one breath away from the Ether and begging me to feed from him. I couldn't do it.

"Night Owl," Skeele says. "You're looking... dirty."

A strange noise escapes my throat, both a cry and soft

laugh. I run toward him and throw my arms around his neck. He hugs me back, cold arms and all.

"I can't stay," he whispers. "I knew I could never stay forever." He presses cold lips to the side of my face.

I nod, noticing he doesn't smell alive. No brimstone and smoke. He doesn't smell like the Skeele I spent all those years with.

"Don't cry, little Night Owl," Skeele says, cool lips against my ear. "We are in the middle of a war."

"They have Rue," I say.

Skeele's expression turns to stone. "Then they must die. Now, tell me how we win this thing."

I release him and turn to face the battlefield. Angels and Hellions and Demons are still fighting. Lucifer is watching us from the sky where he circles like a seagull ready to pounce.

I glance to Sparrow, who nods while pressing his lips into a thin line. I try to think of the best approach but brute force seems to be the only answer.

"Clear us a path to Lucifer," I say.

Shay has a Deacon. Which means I have a Deacon. But this one is different. This one can't die because he already did. I've never loved double jeopardy more than in this moment.

Hope floods my veins like hearing there's a snow day and no school in the morning.

Lucifer lands. Dark eyes focus on me. "I'm waiting, Granddaughter," he shouts over the sound of battle. "If you want your child, come and get her."

Thirty-Four

Jed reached in his bag, scraping off thick, dried mud. He pulled out the jar of feathers Meg had left in his and Shay's safe keeping when she brought Rue and Remington to the Peabody Library.

"Hmm," Jed shifted the jar of feathers, holding it up to Hellsky and letting the ochre din filter through.

"I wonder...." Archaic light twisted from his fingers. He whispered words that sounded like the sweetest lullaby, like the guttural moans of a woman giving birth, like the crackling of sunlight at first dawn.

"What are you doing?" Shay asked, towering over him in her Demon form.

Jed didn't reply. He was too focused, drawing on magic he'd only used once before. Something that was both dark and light, both beautiful and ugly. His aura was glowing Cherenkov radiation. Bright and blue—so bright Shay had to shield her eyes and back away.

Shay had an uneasy feeling. "I think you should stop, Jed," she warned.

He didn't acknowledge that he'd heard her. He'd only done something like this once before when he brought back Nightingale. But it seemed he might have a gift for bringing back the dead. He continued his spellcasting until the jar of feathers transformed into the form of a snowy owl.

The raptor settled on his arm, her dark eyes gazing into his.

"Hello, Elyse, I've heard a little about you," Jed said. "Your mother needs you." He shifted his arm and the owl took flight.

THIRTY-FIVE

Having spent half her life alone and unloved, Meg was having a hard time comprehending the scenes that had unfolded moments ago. Her father, her Hellions, the Crossroads Demon army... it was too much and everything. It filled her with hope. She was not alone in this. She had so many who had come to defeat evil and save Rue. Meg didn't have time for tears now. She reached down for something she'd buried, something she'd held back for years. It was a quick anger, a rage, a hate for those who had wronged her, it had grown even stronger knowing they'd wronged her child.

The battlefield parted, pushed back by Shay's army and Meg's Hellions. Meg went straight for Lucifer who had landed in the clearing, wings spread wide.

"Where is my daughter?" Meg screamed at Lucifer, face twisted in hate. "What have you done with her?"

Meg's heart pounded against her ribs as she raced across the war-torn battlefield. The ground trembled beneath her feet, fractured and steaming from the infernal heat that emanated from the heart of Hell. Crusted mud fell from her body and Sparrow's as he ran beside her.

The clashing of weapons and roars of Demon, the cries of Angels faded into a distant roar as Meg's focus narrowed on Lucifer.

The battlefield spread, leaving a straight path. Shadows twisted away, recoiling from the power that radiated from her, and the jagged earth pulled back, forming a corridor that led straight to Lucifer himself.

Meg's boots pounded against the scorched earth, each step driving her forward, closer to the embodiment of Evil that had stolen her daughter and shattered the fragile hope she'd fought so hard to protect. Her fists were clenched weapons, nails biting in to her palms but she welcomed the pain. It anchored her, fueled the fire burning inside her chest.

Lucifer stood at the far end of the battlefield, his dark wings spread wide, his eyes twin infernos of crimson light. He waited, unbothered, his lips curved in a mocking smile. His presence dominated the world around him, warping the air with raw, suffocating power.

"Come then," he called, his voice echoing with sinister allure. "Face me, little queen. Let's see how strong you really are without your wings."

Meg didn't falter. She drew in a breath, tasting ash and magic, and felt her own power surge to the surface. Her determination crystallized, a molten resolve that burned hotter than Hellfire. This was for Rue. This was for every sacrifice, every piece of herself she'd lost along the way. She would not bow. She would not break.

The path before her began to close, jagged shards of

stone rising up as if to trap her, but Meg kept running, defiant. Energy crackled around her, a wild unchained force that lit up the battle field.

Suddenly, there was a movement in the air, the sound of beating wings, the whisp-hush stroke of feathers, a shallow hoot.

Meg glanced to the side, nearly stumbling when she recognized the snowy owl. Elyse. Fire flooded her veins.

As she drew nearer, the world seemed to hold its breath, a stillness descending over the battlefield that made the hair on the back of her neck stand on end. This was it. She raised her Basilisk tooth and leapt over the debris with a battle cry that echoed for miles.

Lucifer was relentless, his dark wings slicing through the air like jagged shadows. He lunged, his hands crackling with Hellfire. Meg barely managed to dodge it, rolling across the cracked earth. Lucifer stomped and magma broke through the ground with a crack, heat searing her cheek, leaving a blistered line of red.

"Is this all you have, little fallen Queen?" Lucifer taunted, his voice a rich, mocking drawl. He glanced at Sparrow, who had been intersected by a huge Hellion that looked like a boar crossed with an elephant. "So much for the help. Your cursed bird-man can't help you now." He advanced, eyes alight with cruel fire. "I was told an omen ages ago. The Deacons told me the females of my bloodline would kill me." He reached for Meg, grabbed her leg and dragged her closer. "So I've killed them. One by one. But for some reason, you just won't die."

The snowy owl swooped down, talons spread and clawed at Lucifer's face. He dropped Meg's leg with a howl and batted at the owl. But Elyse was quick this time–she remembered the quick swipe of Lucifer's blade and dodged it, flying out of reach before planning her next attack.

Meg gritted her teeth, anger surging through her veins. She lifted her Basilisk tooth blade and lashed out, firelight glinting off the edge with desperate brilliance. The strike connected, cutting Lucifer's arm and sending a spray of dark ichor into the air. But Lucifer only laughed, the wound sealing as quickly as it had opened.

"That tickled," he chuckled.

Meg's eyes went wide as she realized the Basilisk poison did nothing to him.

He retaliated with a brutal backhand, his strength sending Meg crashing to the ground. Pain erupted in her ribs and the impact forced air from her lungs. Stars danced across her vision as she struggled to rise.

A strong hand reached down and dragged her up. It was Skeele, but he was a momentary blur as he went on battling the Demons surrounding them. He moved like a dancer, agile and nimble. The way he pulled Meg to her feet was nothing more than a heavily practiced segment of his routine, reminiscent of the smooth and steady years they'd spent together.

"Stay down," Lucifer commanded, his voice booming. "Your defiance is pathetic. Your unwillingness to die, uncouth."

Meg refused.

Above her, Lucifer loomed, a dark fallen angel? of power and malice. His wings unfurled like a shroud, casting her in shadow. He summoned a spear of black flame, the weapon pulsing with deadly intent.

Meg's legs shook but her will was unbroken. The war raged around them, her allies battling for their lives. For Rue. She couldn't give up. Not now. Not after all she'd been through. Lucifer was nothing more than a dog on a chain with a peanut butter and jelly sandwich.

Lucifer sneered, his eyes narrowing. "Very well. If you wish to die on your feet, so be it."

He lunged, faster than lightning. Meg brought her blade up to meet him. The clash of their powers sent a shockwave through the battlefield, scattering lesser Demons and Angels alike. Lucifer's might was overwhelming, his strength too much for Meg. He drove her back, blow after crushing blow.

Meg's grip on her blade weakened. She stumbled, barely keeping herself upright. Each strike from Lucifer sent agony shooting through her limbs. She spit blood into the dirt.

Meg glanced toward Sparrow, afraid. She was losing, and quickly. This was defeat. All these years she thought she could do this alone. She couldn't. She needed him.

"Meg!" Sparrow's voice cut through the chaos. "Watch out!"

Meg's gaze flicked away for the briefest moment. She only wanted to gaze upon her family and friends one last time before death was delivered to her.

Lucifer struck, his fist colliding with her chest. She was thrown backward, her body slamming into the ground.

The world spun as pain reverberated throughout every bone in her body.

Lucifer approached with merciless, dark aura suffocating the air around her. Meg's hands twitched, struggling to grasp her fallen sword. The edge of despair crept into her heart.

"The Deacons were *wrong*." Lucifer raised his flaming spear.

Meg closed her eyes, bracing herself for the end.

"There isn't room in my back for any more knives. If you're going to kill me, you're going to have to look me in the eyes while you do it," Meg whispered, blood dripping from her mouth. Pain radiated in her ribs. She widened her eyes in challenge and Lucifer paused.

Sparrow grabbed Meg in a violent maneuver, but he couldn't stop the haste. He wrapped her close then knelt, forcing her to the ground underneath him protectively. Then, he collected the darkness within, letting it boil until it was ready to burst. There would be other injuries, maybe even deaths, but he had to do something. He wasn't going to watch her die again. The feathers burst from his wings, a million black razors filled the air directly over them.

———

THE DEACON WATCHED Meg and Lucifer battle with bated breath. He noticed when a cool burst of air approached his side. He turned, detecting the flickering of a ghost breaking through. He recognized the dark hair and red lips. The Deacon smiled. Clea had arrived.

"Now, specter, now is our time," the Deacon said as he raised his hands.

Clea drew upon rage, one that boiled within her when she saw all the ways her father tried to kill the female blood line. She drew upon ancient power, something deep from under the realm of Hell. Something she never knew existed.

She screamed. The Deacon was staring at her, but it didn't stop her as she raised her arms and gathered wind from Hellsky.

The Deacon matched her energy.

Clea and the Deacon blasted the wind in the direction of Sparrow's feathers that were hovering in the air.

The razors from Sparrow's wings hit only one target, the one Clea directed them at, She forced the wind to drive every feathered blade into her father's chest: deep. Into his heart. Into his bones. Into his blackened soul. So deep they would never be removed.

The Deacon smiled proudly. "There you go."

"Grandmother," Remington whispered as he ran toward Clea's flickering form.

But then she was gone. She'd used every ounce of energy that had kept her soul there. She was gone for good, no longer trapped after Alastor had sliced her with iron. The prophecy was half fulfilled.

Sparrow stood, wings nothing more than a skeletal scaffold, watching as Lucifer roared and bled. Meg made a noise, unable to contain the desire to end him once and for all.

Sparrow gripped her arms, he gave her a hard stare. "Your teeth are *sharp*. Your eyes are *luminous*. Everyone will whisper your name in hushed tones after *this*." He nodded then picked her up and ran with her, straight toward Lucifer. Sparrow threw her through the air, launching her like a missile.

Meg didn't have wings but the flight was graceful and strong. The way Hellsky lit up in the background, the way the lightning cracked and energy lit the air, she might as well have had wings burst from her back in that moment.

Meg's feet hit gore-stained dirt. She ran three steps, leapt, climbed up Lucifer's tall body like he was a tree and *bit*. She didn't leave one drop of blood. She drank until he was a husk and his skin turned to ash. She broke his bones, cracked his femurs over her knee, and drank the marrow until they crumbled to dust. She drank until the blades from Sparrow's feathers fell to the ground in a metallic clatter.

"Fuck your omen," she muttered with blood stained lips.

The battleground went silent. The Hellions and Demons that were once noble to Lucifer paused to face their new Queen.

Meg closed her eyes and turned to find every soul on the battleground staring at her. She wiped blood from her mouth and searched the field for her son, then Sparrow. After setting eyes on both of them, she said, "I'm going to get Rue." And turned, running toward what was left of the castle.

Sparrow darted after her, bone tips of what was left of his wings scraping on the ground.

Thirty-Six

Rue lay motionless in the dark, cold dungeon of the castle in the burning caves. Her skin was pale, her breaths shallow.

Dacre knelt beside her, his heart pounding with something he wasn't used to. He couldn't explain it. He knew from the moment the little princess had sunk her teeth into his neck that everything had changed. The handsome Demon, who usually wore arrogance as effortlessly as his black suite, looked uncharacteristically vulnerable. He brushed a strand of hair from Rue's face, his hand trembling. Something had happened to her while he was gone. Dacre scanned her body for injury and concluded, perhaps, it was the blood she'd taken from him. It was changing her and had sent her body into some kind of hibernation state.

The battle above raged on, the sounds of Hellfire and war echoing through the stone walls. He had to get her to safety, incapable of denying the pull to keep her safe. It was too strong, overwhelming. It had kept him awake all night, made him unable to sit or calm his thoughts.

"Come on, Rue," Dacre whispered, his voice horse. "Wake up."

She didn't stir. Her eyelids remained closed, her lashes casting shadows over bruised cheeks. Dacre's jaw clenched. The castle shook. He glanced at the door, remembering the empty cells he'd passed on his way to Rue's. The creatures of the dungeon had been let loose by Lucifer and they were battling above. Rue was alone. The heat from the caves was growing more oppressive as Lucifer's dark force pulsed through the air. Dacre doubted the castle would remain standing much longer.

He stood, carefully gathering Rue in his arms. Her small form was fragile against his chest and he felt a surge of protectiveness that made his blood boil. The battle outside wasn't over yet, but he had a duty now. He had always teetered between alliances. His family was devout to nothing more than the shadows and debts. But all that had changed now.

Dacre made his way out of Rue's cell and through the dungeon's dim corridors. He was wrong when he thought all the creatures had joined the efforts on the battlefield. Demons and hellish beasts lunged at him, desperate to tear them apart. Dacre's eyes flashed dangerously, his nearly human features twisting with fury. Dacre didn't need to fight with a weapon; the claws that appeared from his fingertips was enough to scare the creatures away. The way his face transformed told the story of *what* he was, more formidable than anything housed in the dungeons of the castle in the burning caves. He held Rue close, clutched her small form to his chest until he could feel her shallow breaths against his ribs. He didn't dare wake her now, didn't want her to see him like this.

A monstrous creature with jagged horns leapt from the shadows. Dacre spun, lashing out with one clawed hand, relieving the creature of its head with one rake of his talons. The creature dissolved into ash, leaving the air heavy with the stench of sulfur. Dacre gritted his teeth, his muscles straining as he continued forward, doing his best not to lose control while he held something so precious in his arms. He'd never forgive himself if he harmed her. He had to keep the darkness in check.

Dust sifted through the air as the castle shook again. Stone crumbled. The hallways behind them began collapsing in on themselves. Dacre clutched Rue tighter and moved faster. He ran past stone walls bending and dripping ichor. It was as though the castle itself was bleeding, wounded. The balance between realms was so off that it threatened to destroy everything. Dacre imagined buildings were crumbling in the Seven Kingdoms of Heaven as well. He already knew the Earthen plane burned and shifted with chaos.

Dacre saw the winding stairwell a few feet away. A stone from the ceiling fell, hit his foot and caused him to stumble. He shook off the pain, one goal on his mind.

"Hold on, princess," he murmured, not caring that she couldn't hear him. "We're almost there."

He ran up the stairs that crumbled under his feet. More stone fell. Windows broke and glass sprayed. Dacre ignored the fresh cuts to his face and arms, only glanced down at Rue to ensure she remained unharmed. The glass had cut her cheek. A small dot of blood began to seep out. Dacre shook his head to focus, reached the landing, and began sprinting toward the door that led outside.

The battle outside the castle was a nightmare of chaos and destruction. The landscape of the royal lands had changed, warped by Lucifer's reign and fury. The sky burned with dark flames. Dacre waited in the shadows, Rue cradled protectively in his arms. He watched as Hellions and Angels slaughtered each other. He smiled as the Crossroads Demon girl revealed her own army and the Demonhorse set fire into the sky. His head snapped, refocused on the female voice who cried over the battlefield and demanded Lucifer give back her daughter.

Dacre's chest was heavy. He didn't want to let Rue go. He wanted to take her and run away. He glanced down, focused on the drop of blood on her cheek. A deep growl emanated from his chest.

"Just this once," he promised himself as he dipped his head and licked her wound, savoring the taste of her blood. "Never again."

The cracking of bones echoed across Hellscape and Dacre looked up to see Meg standing over Lucifer's carcass. It was time, she would come for Rue next and nothing would stop her.

Dacre recognized the skeletal wings of the dark Angel who followed Meg. He straightened his back and began walking toward them.

Dacre exited the shadows, carrying Rue toward her mother at an even pace. His arms aching only because he knew he couldn't keep her. He didn't want Meg to see him as threatening, knew that might certainly end his life prematurely. The battle for Hell and balance was over, the war ended, but the tension didn't leave him.

"Give her to me," Meg shouted as she ran closer.

Dacre didn't back down, he did his best to communicate that he was not going to harm Rue.

"She's okay," he said. "I didn't hurt her. I got her out. The castle is going to collapse."

Meg glanced to the burning caves, the smoke replaced with rock dust as the building slowly collapsed in on itself.

"If you hurt her, I will kill you," Meg promised.

Dacre knew she would. "I would never," he said.

The Raven King was eyeing Dacre suspiciously.

Dacre carefully lowered Rue into Meg's waiting embrace. Then he stepped back and dropped to his knee. The Demon's usual cocky demeanor was nowhere to be found. He looked at Meg, his eyes shadowed.

"She'll be okay," he said, though the assurance felt hollow. "I kept her safe." It was mostly true.

Meg didn't reply, her attention wholly on her daughter. She held Rue close, tears streaming down her face, but a flicker of gratitude shone in her eyes as she looked down at Dacre.

"I won't forget this," Meg promised.

Dacre finally let his exhaustion show, his shoulders slumping. The weight of everything he'd done, every choice he'd made, pressed heavily on him. But as he watched Meg hold Rue he knew he'd made the right choice, and for once that was enough. He hated that he'd never see Rue again. She was something he couldn't keep, something not meant for him. Like so much in his world.

Thirty-Seven

Shay stared at the ones whom she'd made Demon pacts with. They were all whole, they hadn't turned into walking sacks of flesh. They were certainly dead but wandering this realm. They were newly dead. The realization came as Shay's figure returned to normal. They'd died. *And out of the strong will come something sweet.* She'd used the power of their souls to change forms, her and Nero both, the pact fulfilled.

"Send their souls away," Chel ordered.

"No," Shay said. "They're *mine*."

"You can't keep them," Chel warned. "They must repent in a Safe House and go to whichever plane they belong on. This is not for you to decide. You'll disrupt the natural order of things. The Deacons will put a bounty on your head."

"Your natural order of things appears to be quite fucked. They are mine. I won't send them away." Shay wasn't about to bow down to Hell or the Seven Kingdoms of Heaven or the Deacons. None of them had done much for her. She glanced around. "There are no Deacons. No Safe Houses," she sneered. "It no longer matters."

"Shay-baby," Jed's voice broke through the chaos of her mind. The Demon poison was spreading the longer she remained in this form. It was changing her, erasing her humanity.

Energy crackled in Jed's fingertips. "You don't want to do this, Shay-baby," Jed said softly. "Remember who you are."

Shay glanced between Chel and Jed. Thousands of waiting faces focused on her, waiting for her next move. The war between Meg and Lucifer was over but a new war raged on in Shay's center. Her soul battled the Demon-poison that had taken over her body.

Shay only saw blackness, power that had boiled to a char during the darkest parts of the war and refused to leave her veins. She wanted to keep it, wanted to marinate in it. She had a power like never before. No one could hurt her now. No one could hurt Nero. The horse whinnied wildly, sensing her thoughts. She was remembering all the terrible things that had happened during her life on the Earthen plane. The taunts from Clyburn, the kidnapping, the death of her parents, the devastation of the family ranch in Montana. Dark power surged through her body. She'd never be weak and human again, never find herself in those situations ever again. Shay smiled darkly.

Nero nudged her shoulder and whinnied softer. He sent a plea down the golden thread that connected their souls. Shay shivered, hated that it was so hard for her to *want* to return back to her human form.

"Shay-baby," Jed said calmly, moving closer, fingers

glowing brighter. "Remember who you are. You aren't this."

Shay gripped her weapon and glanced toward the thousands of souls who waited for her next move. A familiar face stepped forward. Grandmother Crow.

The old woman's expression was one of concern. "Your Daddy wouldn't want this for you," Grandmother Crow said.

She remembered the old woman from her childhood and life in Montana. It seemed so long ago. Grief surged; she didn't want Grandmother Crow to be dead.

Shay rubbed her face and fought the forces warring within her chest. But then, something strange happened. The thousands of souls that stood steady, awaiting her decision to release them or hold them, parted. A white horse walked toward her. Sparkling white. Its mane was glossy and twinkling as though specked with diamonds.

Nero whinnied softly and Shay felt something pure emanate from him.

The white horse stopped in front of Shay. *"So, you are Nero's human."* The white horse tipped its head to the side, inspecting her. *"You're not looking very human right now. I've been watching you, Shay. Watching you for a long time. You've been very brave. But this is not what your soul wants. You know this, cowgirl."*

Shay's eyes were wide, she'd never heard a horse speak before. Something throbbed in her chest trying to get out. It clawed at her throat.

"I can't let them go," Shay whispered, her eyes wide.

"You want to let them go, Shay-baby," the white horse said. *"You don't want this darkness. You are good."* The

white horse searched Shay's blackened eyes. *"You are the wind that races lightning over the Montana prairie. You are sunlight and wildflowers. Not this."*

Jed was close enough to stop her; a spell was waiting on his tongue, his fingertips glowing with magic.

"Shay-baby," the white horse said, *"Come back to us as you were."*

In the space between heartbeats, Shay changed back into her human form and collapsed on her knees. She was crying–exhausted, but free.

Jed picked her up and held her close. Nero nuzzled Shay's shoulder.

"I'm so sorry," Shay whispered. "I don't know what happened."

"You helped save us," Jed said.

Everyone turned as the castle in the burning caves came tumbling down in a thundering roar.

Thirty-Eight

"I kept her safe, like you asked," Skeele said, voice full of emotion. "But it was so much more. More than I ever thought I'd have. More than I ever thought I deserved. A Demon from the hovels..." he shook his head, a tear beading the corner of his eye.

Sparrow's expression was blank and he only glanced at Meg exactly once, his arms tightening on Rue as he passed the unconscious girl to her brother. Remington carried her with ease and Nightingale fussed, delving into her dreams to wake her.

"She'll be mad that you asked me to watch over her," Skeele continued. "But it was my duty." He patted over his heart. "It was my greatest honor."

Skeele turned to Rue and Remington. "You've both grown so much in such a short time. Too much, really. And I'm sure by now you know the truth. I'm not your father." His expression faltered to one of regret.

"Yes, you were," Remington said as he set a now awake Rue on her feet.

Rue threw her arms around Skeele, unsteady on her feet after being woken from such a deep sleep. "Of course you were," she whispered. "We never got to say goodbye."

Something meowed from Skeele's pocket. "Oh," he smiled. "I found this." He pulled Lucipurr out and handed the kitten to Rue. "He told me he belonged to you. I found him biting a little Demon. Seems he wanted to join in on the battle."

"You can speak to cats?" Rue asked, tucking the kitten in her pocket.

"Cats walk the edges of the realms. They talk in an old dialect of Hellspeak. They're half in." Skeele smiled.

"You're going away?" Remington asked.

"Yes," Skeele nodded. "I can't stay here." He hugged Rue then Remington then Thrush. He shook Sparrow's hand and patted his elbow. "Take care of them." He stood in front of Meg and smiled softly. "Be nice." He kissed her cheek, his eyes falling to the missing wings behind her shoulders. "You're looking very human these days. It suits you. The wings were kinda preposterous." He smiled.

Meg's face was twisted in sorrow. She scanned his face, unbelieving he was there. Unbelieving that she had another moment with him. There was so much she wanted to say but none of it would pass her lips.

"I love you too, Night Owl," Skeele smiled. "I wish we'd had more time." He glanced to Sparrow. "But you were never fully mine. We both know that."

A whimper escaped Meg's throat as she reached for him, one last hug for the man she knew she didn't deserve. Every memory flashed through her mind as though she were dying right along with him. But, this wasn't death, no this was rebirth. She kissed the corner of his mouth, scratching at his clothing as it began slipping through her fingertips.

"I'm going now." Skeele waved and winked, then faded away to nothing.

Meg threw herself at Sparrow, sobbing like never before crying like she'd never ever let herself do. The deep sobs wracked her ribs and made a terrible sound in her throat and echoed over the silent battlefield.

Sparrow rubbed her back and buried his face in the crook of her neck. He folded skeletal wings around them both, bent his knees and took her to the ground on his lap. He held her tighter than ever before. He would never let her go. He would spend the rest of his life keeping her safe, protecting her, groveling for the hurt he'd caused in the name of balance for the realms. He hated that he'd hurt her to protect her. Never again.

"I told you…," Sparrow whispered in Meg's ear, "I told you we'd be invincible together." He wiped ichor from her shoulder and kissed the soft space over her collarbone.

THIRTY-NINE

The hallways of Sparrow's house were quiet, the echoes of recent battles still lingering in everyone's minds. For days everyone had slept and ate and hid in shadows.

Meg moved silently though the corridor, her steps heavy, heart caught between a pang of sadness she couldn't quite shake and relief.

Jed walked beside her, his expression shadowed and conflicted. He didn't like what Meg had asked of him, and though he'd agreed, the unease in his eyes was hard to miss.

"She's sleeping," Meg said as she reached for the door handle to Rue's room. "I checked on her earlier." She opened the door.

Rue's dark hair spilled wild over the pillow, her forehead creased in dreaming. Rue's breaths were rapid as though she were running. Meg couldn't shake the memories of Rue's broken sobs and her wide, haunted eyes. The darkness that lingered in Rue's gaze was something Meg couldn't bear to see.

Teari had seen the girl and uneasily blamed the crying and haunted expression on the war and the kidnapping. But Rue continued to walk the halls of Sparrow's house with haunted eyes, waking the house frequently at night with screams from nightmares that no one could wake her from. It needed to end. And Meg only knew of one way to help her daughter.

Jed moved closer to the bed, his hand hovering uncertainly at his side.

"Are you sure, Meg?" His voice was rough. "What if she asks questions? Figures out something's missing?"

Meg's gaze didn't waver. "I'd rather she has a gap than live with those memories. Look what it's doing to her. She's too young for that darkness." Meg's eyes softened as she looked back at Rue, sadness clutching her throat. She'd promised herself that her children wouldn't see trauma like she'd endured in her childhood. Meg had promised to keep her children safe and she'd failed with Rue. She needed to fix it.

"Please," Meg begged Jed. "Just since the kidnapping, that's it. Leave everything else. We can work around a few days missing from her memory."

Jed swallowed and gave a slow nod. He'd seen memories etched in blood, trauma carved into minds so deeply that no spell could ease them. Rue was young, her spirit hadn't taken in that darkness fully. He hoped, at least, that it hadn't.

Jed stepped closer to the bed and lifted his hands, his fingers glowing faintly as his magic rose from his center and began to pulse through the room. Since the war, he'd become much stronger. The air felt heavy, charged. Jed closed his eyes and whispered words that sounded like the falling petals of a rose, the gentle lapping of dark lake water in the moonlight, the foggy sunrise on an autumn day. He found the memories that tormented Rue's mind; the cold stone of the dungeon, the chains, Hellions, the Demons that had looked at her with hungry eyes, the taste of blood on her tongue, and... a handsome Demon. Jed wiped it. Memories gone. Blank slate.

As the spell settled, Rue shifted slightly in sleep, her small hand clenching and then relaxing as Jed's magic wove gently around her mind. Rue's breathing relaxed, the creases in her expression faded to a peaceful, almost angelic expression.

Jed lowered his hands, the glow around them fading. He took a step back, exhaustion settling into his features.

"It's done," he said quietly, his voice thick with the strain of the magic he'd used. The aura around him pulsed blue light. "She won't remember any of it. All she'll remember is looking for the kitten that morning and waking up on the battlefield after the defeat."

Meg nodded. "Thank you."

Jed paused, before telling Meg about the handsome Demon and the blood-drinking that had been forced upon Rue at the Black Mansion.

Meg's features shifted as anger threatened to overtake her. She closed her eyes and took a deep breath before saying, "Never tell a soul. Erase your own memories of this moment if you need to. But never, ever speak of this."

They left Rue to sleep undisturbed and walked back to the living room where Teari and Shay waited.

Teari looked worried. "Did you do it?"

Jed nodded.

Teari sighed and walked toward Meg, pulling her into her arms. "I'm sorry we couldn't find another way to help her. I think this is the right thing to do."

Meg smiled softly and gripped her friends' hands. "I know you tried. You always have."

FORTY

EARLY DAWN STRETCHED ACROSS THE VAST, untouched grasslands of the Earthen plane, the world now quiet and still. Sunlight seeped over the horizon, casting hues of amber and soft pink across tall grasses creating a warm glow. All of it undisturbed by darkness, finally. Nero stood poised, muscles coiled and tense as though he still had to prepare himself for the weight of the past. Nearby, the white horse watched, her gaze serene.

For the first time in what felt like ages, they had no destination, no battle calling them, no shadows tracking their every move. They no longer moved through the realms like wisp on the periphery.

For Nero, calls to the Crossroads had slowed. For the white horse, the pursuit of others trying to find her dissipated like the wind. There was open sky and endless earth before them. The tears in the Veil had become so small, they had to search for hours before finding one for crossing into the Seven Kingdoms of Heaven or Hell.

Nero took a step, feeling the softness of the earth

beneath his hooves. He surged forward, his mane streaming behind him like a dark banner, hooves thundering against the earth as he raced nothing more but the sunlight. The white horse bolted beside him, graceful and sure, keeping pace with an effortless stride. Her whinny of joy echoed in his ears.

They ran as if they were the wind, two figures who belonged wholly to the wild. Nero veered toward a hill and the white horse followed, their breath visible in the cool morning air. When they reached the summit, Nero halted, looking over the stretch of land that lay below; the valleys and rivers winding toward the horizon like threads in a vast tapestry. He recognized this place, wandered until he found where he had been left by his mother. Tucked away under scrub brush, this was the tiny corner of land where Shay had found him covered in bees and barely alive.

The white horse nudged him, her eyes gleaming with quiet understanding.

"It was not chance that she found you," she whispered as though it were the simplest truth. *"It was not chance that she nursed you back to life."* The white horse circled him.

HE'D ONLY BEEN BORN a few hours earlier, dropped in the prairie grass by a mare who wasn't sure raising a foal in the offseason was such a good thing. When the bees came out of the ground and swarmed on her, she ran. She left him to die, wet and cold. But the warm Montana sun dried the wetness from his coat and mane, and he rose up on knobby-kneed legs only to be stung over and over again.

Shay wasn't much more than a teenager when she

pointed to the black foal in the distance. It didn't take much to convince Nicholas to take the foal home. Shay lifted him, draping the small horse over her lap as she rode back to the ranch.

WHAT NERO DIDN'T KNOW WAS that Shay saw the white horse first. She'd followed the white horse like a mirage and was led to Nero.

Nero broke into a gallop, the white horse matching his speed. They splashed through a river, cold water spraying around them before veering into a thick grove of pines where shafts of light filtered down, illuminating their path like a blessing. They didn't stop; they ran until the landscape blurred, until every memory felt like a distant dream. Each step took them further from the darkness that had once bound them.

And as the sun rose higher, they continued, two spirits, wild and free, their whinnies echoing through the fields, untouchable and unconquered. The white horse was now able to carry on in the realm that was her land. Her peace. There was finally balance.

"Do you want to go home?" the white horse asked.

"Yes," Nero said, finally tired of running.

"Let's go home to Shay," the white horse said, and they turned toward Montana and the ranch that Shay and Jed were rebuilding.

FORTY-ONE

MEG

WALKING through these hallways has become familiar, calming. There are no shadows for dark creatures to hide and slither. No Hellions roaming the halls looking for danger. I pause outside Sparrow's bedroom door. We've been discussing rebuilding Hell and in the coming days we'll need to return. Thankfully Sparrow has experience rebuilding a kingdom even if it's on a different realm. Heaven isn't that far from Hell.

I look forward to building a new home, something that suits us both. I smile to myself. What chaos we will bring to the realms; half-darkness, half-light, intermingling in realms we don't belong in. Too bad. Those Archangels will have to eat a dick because after fighting for our lives against Lucifer, I'm never listening to a single one of them ever again. My stomach grumbles and the door whips open.

Sparrow glances down at me, grabs my hand, and drags me inside his room.

"You're hungry," he mutters.

"I was gonna make some spaghetti," I say.

Sparrow smirks. "I'm hungry."

"I didn't know you liked spaghetti."

"Maybe get some Twinkies." He smiles. "Or pizza. Or those blasphemous snowball things you eat that make a holy mess."

"Those are delicious. Don't hate on the snowballs." I shake my head and consider biting him for talking shit about my junk food. "You don't keep that stuff in the house and Noah refuses to find me food after what we put Thrush through. Especially since I gave him freedom."

Sparrow's brow rises. "Thrush did what he wanted to do. We couldn't have stopped him. He hated it here and told us so each and every day."

I shrug. "I know. I just hope he's feeding the Basilisk."

Sparrow shakes a finger at me. "That is why Noah is mad at you. He hates those things."

"They're good to have around."

He scans me for a moment, licks his lips, and says, "I guess I'll just have you then."

I glance at Sparrow's bony scaffold of wings. Small, black feathers are starting to grow in.

Sparrow shudders, holding in a tic of madness that threatens to wrack his whole body.

"Is it back?" I ask, worried.

Sparrow holds up his finger, his jaw clenching and eyes closed as he tries to control it. He sits on the edge of the bed and grips his knees, leaning forward. His teeth grind.

"I'm fine," he finally says.

Green eyes flash open and the dark haze clears.

"Is it bad like before?" I ask.

"No." He grabs the waistband of my jeans and drags me closer, between his legs, trapping me.

I thread my fingers through his hair and massage his scalp.

He kneads my back and hips, wraps his arms around my waist and presses his face to my stomach. We just hold each other like this for minutes. And I remember how he looked in battle... graceful and elegant and absolutely fucking lethal. He is mine and I am his. Both of us half-dark and half-light; mine born and bred, his by torment and curses and honor. We have been broken and reborn. Hated and loved. The cycle of chaos ends here, like that birthmark. Little did I know Alastor was doing me a favor when he made me cut the birthmark off my leg. When I find him again, I might thank him.

Sparrow's arm snakes around my waist, pulling me closer, nuzzling his face into my stomach.

"I hear you," he whispers. "Are you ever not hungry?"

I grip his hair and pull at the roots until his head tips back and we make eye contact. I lick my lips. He's never looked better than he does right now, staring up at me.

"I still haven't forgiven you for what you did to my book." Sparrow blinks slowly.

"Which book?" I ask.

"Birds of Paradise."

Damn. That was a long time ago. I stole it from his house and dragged it all over Hellscape. It was dropped in the mud and covered in food. Hmm. It's probably gone for good, destroyed when the castle in the burning caves collapsed.

"Well…" I release a small huff that sounds like a laugh. "I guess you have the next best thing."

"Oh yeah, what's that?" he asks.

"We are birds of paradise."

He smiles and nods, slowly agreeing before he presses the side of his face to my belly again, wrapping his arms so tight I can barely breath and begins to hum *Bed of Roses*.

There he is. There's my old Sparrow Man. I've finally got him back.

———

THERE IS A FEATHER, sparkling and golden. Of all places, it's resting inconspicuously on the bathroom countertop. I hesitate. I haven't received a feather in years. It could be nothing. It could be *something*.

I reach forward, finger pointed. An arc of electricity connects with the tip. My eyes widened and I suck in a breath. My knees buckle. I grip the counter. Blood turns to ice in my veins.

There is a thud from the bedroom. Maybe he senses the feather. He's always had a knack for that. Sparrow tries the handle, then bangs on the door.

"What's happened?" he asks, breaking the handle and shoving the door open, eyes wide in fear. I guess that's what happens after all we've been through.

I fake a smile and brush the feather down the drain. I turn the water on for good measure and drown it.

"Nothing." I smile. "Everything is fine. Just fine. Never better."

I'll be damned if I let a fucking feather ruin my life ever again.

-The End-

Afterword

From the Author.

Wow. I can hardly believe I just typed "The End" on Meg and Sparrow's story. After 10 years of writing this, it is bittersweet giving them an ending. After all I've put them through, I think they deserved it. After Veil of Shadows 4: Raven King and Veil of Shadows 6: Night Owl, we were so disappointed in Sparrow and his separation from Meg. But, they had things to do, people to see, lives to live/ruin, and hearts to break.

Even though this is the end, you might still have some questions about people we've met. While Meg and Sparrow's storyline is done, the Veil of Shadows world will live on in at least 4 planned spinoff standalone books. The first will be Rue and Dacre's story. This will be a standalone New Adult Dark Fantasy Romance titled: "The Sky is Starless." It is scheduled to release in the spring of 2025. Follow me on the blog and/or social media and never miss a release!

Special thanks to my editor Kristy, who has been

through the thick and thin of it with this series. She's seen all the "neck ass" and "eye shits" and improperly used "?" and repeating repeating repeating words/phrases, yet, she's stuck with me! Thank you Kristy, for all your editing prowess through the years!

PREVIEW: THE SKY IS STARLESS BY M. R. PRITCHARD

REMINDER: THIS IS AN UNEDITED DRAFT PREVIEW

———

Her memories were stolen.
Her nightmares won't let her forget.
And now, the shadows are coming for her.

Caught between worlds, Rue fights to unravel the truth of her past while resisting the dark pull of Dacre, the one man she shouldn't trust—but can't stay away from. Love was never meant to be easy, but for Rue, it could be deadly.

You can't outrun your bloodline... or the shadows it casts.

Rue is determined to live a normal life, far from the dark legacy of her family. College is supposed to be her fresh start —a chance to blend in, bury her secrets, and maybe even discover who she truly is. But when shadowy figures begin stalking her and nightmares plague her nights, normalcy slips further out of reach.

Her parents' solution? A bodyguard.

Nothing could be more infuriating than Dacre, the mysterious, maddeningly handsome man assigned to shadow her every move. Rue's stubborn streak refuses to make it easy for him—until she notices her nightmares quiet when he's near, and when shadow demons attack, Dacre sends them back to the darkness with startling ease.

Rue's missing memories hold the answers she needs, but everyone—including Dacre—seems determined to keep her in the dark.

Dark secrets.
Forbidden love.
A battle for her soul.

The Sky is Starless is a spellbinding dark fantasy romance perfect for fans of supernatural intrigue, steamy tension, and heroines fighting for their destiny.

———

Chapter One

Early morning light was creeping through the blinds like unwelcome fingers. Rue watched the coffee maker brew, steam rising from the dark liquid as it streamed into a Hedwig mug. It made her think of smoke and dark magic. Of fire and brimstone. Her vision blurred. Rue blinked a few times but it was too late, her mind was going elsewhere... drifting. The stream of coffee turned to thick blood. It dripped in slow, deliberate rivulets, each drop echoed in the small kitchen. *Drip. Drip. Drip.* Rue's throat felt dry. Sweat beaded her forehead as last night's nightmare's resurfaced, she was drowning, gurgling on blood but so *so* thirsty. Rue gripped the edge of the counter, willing the memory to pass.

"It's not real," she whispered, her voice soft, her heart thumping against her ribs. Rue squeezed her eyes shut and shook her head, trying to erase the phantom sensations: the taste of iron, the warmth spreading down her throat, filling her stomach until it no longer ached. It was all so real and it felt *too* good.

Rue rubbed her eyes until she saw stars. When she opened them again, the coffee maker had stopped and the mug sat innocently on the counter. The owl stared back at her, unmarred. The counter was dry and there was no blood in sight. The mug was filled with dark brown liquid, not red. Rue licked her lips and her stomach growled in protest.

Her hands trembled as she reached for the mug, but... she paused, couldn't shake the feeling of being watched. A shadow passed the edge of her vision. Turning slowly, Rue scanned the empty kitchen, her heart racing.

Nothing.

She blew out a nervous breath and muttered to herself, "There is nothing here. No Demons. No Angels. Just you, Rue. Nothing else. No blood. No monsters."

She took milk from the fridge and a spoon from the drawer. She sat with the coffee mug near the window, opened the blinds and watched the sun rise the rest of the way. Rue's leather messenger bag was in the chair next to her. She opened it and took out her planner. She had class in a few hours. Midterms later in the week. She turned the page as she sipped the coffee and glanced out the window again, watching the oak tree drop orange leaves.

She shivered. Although she wasn't cold, it was the understanding that she'd have to leave this world soon and visit home for the winter break. She just wondered if it would be Heaven or Hell and if the dreams would follow her.

———

Chapter Two

Shower steam fogged the tiny bathroom of Rue's apartment. She stepped out, wrapped herself in a towel and reached for the door to let the steam out. Something written on the mirror caught her eye.

A message: *Meet me at the Coffee Connection at two.*

Rue swiped her finger over the message and got ready.

She chose jeans, sneakers, and a chunky black cable knit sweater. She loosely braided her hair to keep it under control with the wind.

Rue slung her leather bag over her shoulder and locked the door to her apartment. She lived in a little brick Tudor style house, that had been converted into two apartments. One above an done below. Her parents had bought the house for Rue to live in, but when Rue argued that it was too much space for just her and the kitten, it was magically renovated. Rue took the upstairs one since she liked the view of the trees and surrounding Loyola campus. The downstairs one was rented quite possibly to a ghost because she never saw the person, only heard the occasional creaks and door squeals. She never saw anyone coming or going, never saw packages get delivered, never heard a vacuum running. She had hoped the person living down there wasn't a complete pig. But, she figured she'd smell something if they were.

Rue jogged down the stairs and passed her car, opting to walk to class since the weather was nice.

*

Rue slid into her usual seat near the back of the lecture hall. The room was already buzzing with conversation, students flipping through notebooks and idly tapping on laptops.

Professor Camden, a wiry man with round glasses and patches sewn over the edges of his brown suitcoat strode into the room. He clapped his hands together, voice booming with too much energy for the hour. "Good morning, everyone! Today, we're diving into the mysteries of the Zapotec civilization!"

Rue opened her notebook, clicked her pen but the tip hovered over the page. Professor Camden's voice became a distant drone as her mind wandered.

A soft tap on her arm pulled her back. She turned to see Evelyn, her perpetually cheerful classmate, grinning like she had a secret.

"Hey, Rue. We're all going to Justin's party tonight. You should come." She swiped at blonde fringe before pressing a Chapstick to her lips.

Rue hesitated, grip tightening on her pen. "I don't know." She hated parties, she found it too hard to relax and have fun. She blamed it on the way she was raised which was not on the Earthen plane.

"Oh, come on!" Evelyn pouted. "You never come to these things. Just for a little while, okay? It'll be fun."

Rue forced a small smile. "I'll think about it."

"No," Evelyn pressed. "You will come. It's the last Halloween party of the season. You haven't seen any of my costumes this year."

Rue's cheeks flushed. "But... I don't have a costume."

"Good. I'll bring one for you." Evelyn winked. "I've got the perfect one. See you at six."

Rue grabbed Evelyn's sleeve and looked her dead in the eyes.

"What?" Evelyn asked.

"It better not be... slutty," Rue warned.

Evelyn smiled widely. "No promises."

Rue slipped out of class as soon as it ended, her bag slung over her shoulder. The campus buzzed with the energy of students heading to lunch, Rue felt like she was moving through a different world. One she didn't belong in. The feeling was what held her back from campus parties and dates and fully putting herself out in the world. The thing was, she didn't belong in this world. She didn't even belong in this realm. She watched people walk by her, none of them had any clue that they were so close to a princess of another realm. Rue shuddered at the thought. She had stopped thinking of herself as a princess a long time ago. Now she was simply Rue. Rue the runaway. Rue the atypical who chose a life in the Earthen plane amongst the normies. She fidgeted with her dark braid and raised her face to the cool breeze. Even if she didn't belong here, it did feel like home.

The Coffee Connection was a typical college town coffee shop with alternative music playing low on the sound system and a sagging couch in the back corner that no one in their right might should ever sit on.

A bell hanging over the door jingled as Rue stepped inside, greeted by the smell of roasted coffee beans.

"Welcome to the Coffee Connection," a barista called from behind the counter.

Rue waved and smiled before scanning the shop.

There she was. Short-cropped black hair and bright blue eyes hidden behind big sunglasses, and legs twice as long as Rue's. One thing Rue didn't inherit from her mother was height.

Meg, her mother, waved and motioned for Rue to come to the small table she'd chosen near the window. Rue went and Meg stood and pulled her in for a hug.

"Rue, I've missed you," she whispered like it was a secret.

"We met here last week," Rue reminded her.

She sat, crossed her long legs and took off her leather jacket. She was wearing a wide necked T-shirt, scars and tattoos marred her arms and shoulders.

A man walked by and did a double take, spilling hot coffee on his hand.

She received looks and stares a lot and Rue was unsure how she ignored it all.

Meg slid a mug toward Rue. "I got you the pumpkin spice latte. I hope that's okay?"

"It's perfect. Thank you," Rue said as she sat and scooted closer. The woman was slightly overbearing at times, but she was Rue's mother.

Rue sipped at her coffee and remembered why she'd limited the meetings and moved away from home. They were too close, she needed distance. Rue needed to get out and find her own place in the world. She had to stop living in the shadow of her parents. She had to get away from the secrets and lies.

"Have you been drinking the bagged blood?" Meg whispered and touched Rue's face. "You look pale."

"I don't need it. I'm fine." Rue plucked the menu off the table and considered a pecan muffin.

"I thought I was fine when I was your age too." Meg frowned. "Your father is worried. He wants you to come home."

"And you?" Rue asked.

"I want you safe. Hidden. But... happy." She stared at Rue. "Would you tell me if something was wrong?"

"Sure." Rue rubbed her arm and pushed away the thoughts of the song from her nightmares that had interrupted every moment of peace.

"You seem distracted."

"I have exams this week." Rue sipped at the coffee. "It's just stress. I promise"

"Did you pick a major?" She asked.

"A long time ago." Rue chuckled. "Archaeology."

"Oh, you did say that. I forgot. Sorry." Meg nodded. "Just don't... do anything dangerous. I'm glad you didn't choose criminal justice or healthcare." She shook her head. "I don't want you in more danger."

"Mother." Rue rolled her eyes. "I can handle myself. I'm fine. Nothing has happened for years and years and years. I'm not in any danger."

There was a pregnant pause. She didn't bring up Angels or Demons because it would be wrong to discuss them in a coffee shop amongst normal humans. But, it wasn't that long ago when her mother sent Rue away to live with her Aunt Shay and Uncle Jed while she saved the world as they knew it. No one here would know anything about that though.

The man was still staring. He'd sat at the table behind them, his eyes focused on Meg's back and the two vertical scars that marred her shoulder blades.

Meg touched Rue's long, braided hair. "I know you can take care of yourself. Remm wants to see you."

"I'll be back for holiday break," Rue reminded her.

"Maybe call him?" she suggested. "I think he likes talking to you. Maybe you could convince him to find a girlfriend."

"I have called him. He never answers." Rue sipped at her coffee. "Why does he bother having a phone if he never answers? Plus, he could come visit me."

"He's been busy..." Meg bit her lip and looked away. "I'll tell you more about it when you come home to visit. This isn't the place to discuss such things."

"Sure." Rue checked her phone, nope not one reply from her brother to any of the text messages she'd sent him last week. She showed Meg, then lowered her voice before asking, "Where are we having the holidays this year? Heaven or Hell?"

Meg smiled wide. "Hell, of course. You know those fucking Angels will ruin every peaceful moment with some shit-fuckery."

Rue laughed, seeing her mother's sharpness reveal itself. She always tried to hide it but every now and then it escaped when everyone least expected it. Dry humor and lots of swearing, she always made Rue laugh.

"What?" Meg scoffed innocently. "You know they will. How is Lucipurr?"

Lucipurr was Rue's cat. A little black kitten with green eyes that her brother had found and brought her when they were kids. The kitten never seemed to grow much, but was smart and friendly and everything Rue needed in a companion.

Rue was still nodding in agreement at the shit-fuckery comment when she replied, "He still acts like a kitten, hiding and escaping." Rue glared at the man behind her mother's shoulder and he noticed, his eyes went wide before he looked away.

Too late. Meg noticed. She leaned back and sipped at her coffee before saying, "You know, this city isn't what it used to be. People used to have respect." She shifted in her seat, turning to face the man and smiled, flashing sharp teeth.

He startled, spilling his coffee. Dark liquid spread across the table and into his lap. "Jesus Christ," he muttered, looking around.

"Meg?" a barista shouted from behind the counter.

She stood and walked toward the counter. The barista passed her a bag.

"Thank you. My husband really loves these," Meg said.

"You tell us every week." The barista was smiling wide, smitten with her. She must've left a big tip.

Rue sighed, assumed that's what a Queen can do. Throw money around willy-nilly, dress like a biker instead of royalty. Rue smiled as she sipped at the pumpkin spice latte and watched the orange and yellow leaves tumble across the sidewalk. Her gaze drifted across the street. The shadows moved just a little too deliberately. She squinted her eyes as it lingered just long enough to send a shiver down her spine.

This Title Releases Spring 2025

About the Author

M. R. Pritchard delves into the profound clash between good and evil, the mystical realms of gods and monsters, and the intricate transformations of ordinary people into beings of immense power. Her gripping narratives often unfold within the haunting backdrop of apocalyptic or post-apocalyptic landscapes, offering a unique blend of suspense and wonder.

M. R. Pritchard is a two-time Kindle Scout winning author, her short story "Glitch" has been featured in the 2017 winter edition of THE FIRST LINE literary journal. Her short story "Moon Lord" has been featured in Chronicle Worlds: Half Way Home (Part of the Future Chronicles) and will be time capsuled on the moon on the Lunar Codex in 2024.

Visit her website MRPritchard.com and Subscribe. You'll get subscriber only content, deleted scenes, updates, special previews of new projects, and book deals.

Veil of Shadows Series:

Sparrow Man

Nightingale Girl

Scarecrow

Raven King

Nightjar

Night Owl

Etched in Darkness

Embrace the Night

Shadows of Destiny

Midnight Serenade

Echoes of Treachery

Omens of Darkness

Thread the Bone

Fantasy/Fairy Tale Love Story/Romance:

Muse

Forgotten Princess Duology

Midsummer Night's Dream: A Game of Thrones

Poetry/Short Stories

Consequence of Gravity